A
Midsummer
Night's
Scream

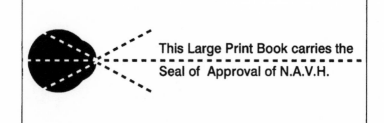

A Jane Jeffry Mystery

A
Midsummer
Night's
Scream

Jill Churchill

Thorndike Press • Waterville, Maine

Published in 2005 by arrangement with William Morrow, an imprint of HarperCollins Publishers Inc.

Thorndike Press® Large Print Core.

The tree indicium is a trademark of Thorndike Press.

The text of this Large Print edition is unabridged. Other aspects of the book may vary from the original edition.

Set in 16 pt. Plantin by Minnie B. Raven.

Printed in the United States on permanent paper.

Library of Congress Cataloging-in-Publication Data

Churchill, Jill, 1943–
    A midsummer night's scream: a Jane Jeffry mystery / by Jill Churchill.
        p. cm. — (Thorndike press large print core)
    ISBN 0-7862-7279-1 (lg. print : hc : alk. paper)
    1. Jeffry, Jane (Fictitious character) — Fiction.
2. Women detectives — Illinois — Chicago — Fiction.
3. Actors — Crimes against — Fiction. 4. Caterers and catering — Fiction. 5. Chicago (Ill.) — Fiction.
6. Theater — Fiction. 7. Large type books. I. Title.
II. Thorndike Press large print core series.
PS3553.H85M53 2005
  813'.54—dc22   2004025410

For my brother, actor and producer John David Young, who helped me with advice, some of which I had to ignore. All mistakes are mine.

National Association for Visually Handicapped

serving the partially seeing

As the Founder/CEO of NAVH, the only national health agency solely devoted to those who, although not totally blind, have an eye disease which could lead to serious visual impairment, I am pleased to recognize Thorndike Press* as one of the leading publishers in the large print field.

Founded in 1954 in San Francisco to prepare large print textbooks for partially seeing children, NAVH became the pioneer and standard setting agency in the preparation of large type.

Today, those publishers who meet our standards carry the prestigious "Seal of Approval" indicating high quality large print. We are delighted that Thorndike Press is one of the publishers whose titles meet these standards. We are also pleased to recognize the significant contribution Thorndike Press is making in this important and growing field.

Lorraine H. Marchi, L.H.D.
Founder/CEO
NAVH

* Thorndike Press encompasses the following imprints: Thorndike, Wheeler, Walker and Large Print Press.

Chapter One

Jane and Shelley were on their way to pillage the grocery store. It was the hottest, most awful July week anyone in the suburbs of Chicago could remember. Jane, who was driving, had a long list of things to acquire. She'd planned out a whole week of cold salads for herself and her kids Mike, Katie, and Todd. Hearty, interestingly shaped pastas, lots of good veggies, hard-boiled eggs, tuna, and chicken to pile upon huge amounts of crisp, cold lettuce, accompanied by big pitchers of iced tea, a twelve-pack of V8, and soft drinks. Frozen fruit desserts. Even Popsicles.

It would only entail one miserable early morning of boiling and sautéing and running up the air-conditioning bill. Then she wouldn't do any real cooking at all until there was a relatively cool day.

"What was wrong with that space right in front of the exit door?" Shelley complained as Jane cruised the grocery store parking lot.

"A beat-up car was next to it. That's the sort of person you don't want to park next to. They don't care about the condition of your car because they don't care about their own."

"You don't intend to park way down the street, where we have to run the carts half a mile and then bring them back, do you?"

"Nope. See the space between the Mercedes and the Land Rover? That's where we want to be — next to people who care about their automobile's well-being."

When they came out of the store, each of them had four bags in her cart. They put them in the back of Jane's Jeep, which she'd equipped with a clear plastic sheet to prevent spills staining the carpet.

"Jane, you're more protective of this Jeep than you were of your children."

"Yes," Jane admitted.

When Jane pulled into her new driveway, noting how nice it was not to have to dodge the horrible pothole anymore, Shelley asked, "What have you heard about your manuscript?"

"You're not supposed to keep asking me about it. I'll tell you later, when we've sorted out which bags belong to each of us and put away the food."

"I haven't asked about your book for a full month. I've kept track," Shelley said, then added, "I have something to talk to you about, too. A new project for us to try out."

Jane almost groaned. In a couple of years they'd be stay-at-home mothers without children at home anymore. They had tried out several jobs and hobbies they had thought would be interesting and profitable. They'd taken on knitting and gardening and took a lot of classes. They'd even attempted to be wedding planners. None of which had claimed their hearts. Jane half feared that if she sold this book and continued to write mysteries, Shelley might not have found a job she also loved.

On the other hand, she might still be able to work with Shelley — most writers probably managed to have a real life and do other things, she assumed.

They managed to sort out which bags were Jane's and which were Shelley's, and when they started taking them inside, Shelley called across their adjoining driveways, "We'll talk about your book and my project over a good dinner out."

"Why would we go out to dinner when we have three tons of food?"

"Because Paul's out of town examining the books of one of his franchised restaurants. He thinks they're fudging the numbers. And all our kids are going to the swimming pool and eating there this evening. You don't want to cook for yourself and neither do I."

"You have a good point. Chinese?"

"Okay."

While they nibbled on crab Rangoon and the best spring rolls in their suburb, Jane told Shelley that Felicity Roane, the nice, helpful writer whom they'd met at a mystery convention, had read her manuscript and made a few suggestions. "I fixed them in two days and sent the manuscript to Melody Johnson. That was three weeks ago." Melody Johnson was the editor whom Felicity Roane had suggested. Jane had met Melody at the same mystery conference and had had an interview with her about her book. Melody had been interested and had asked Jane to send the whole manuscript to her.

"Why didn't you tell me?"

"I was afraid she wouldn't like it and I'd be back at square one."

"Have you heard back from her?"

"No, not yet. I rushed it a bit. I wanted to get it in by the middle of July. I understand publishing pretty well shuts down in August. Everybody goes to the Hamptons or Maine."

"Everybody? They turn off the lights and computers and go away?"

"Not quite. The secretaries and junior editors have to stick around, I imagine. I wanted Melody to have the manuscript before she disappeared on her vacation."

As their Mongolian beef arrived and the appetizer plates, looking as if they'd been licked clean, were taken away, Jane asked, "So what's this project you have in mind?"

"It started when Paul purchased a run-down theater, thinking he could renovate it into a place to keep food supplies for all his restaurants in the Chicago area."

"So?"

"He started getting bids for cleaning it up. And it appeared to be too expensive. He's even more obsessed by cleanliness of food storage than the government agencies are. He'd have had to tear the building down and start from scratch. He didn't want to make the investment in doing that, much less waste the time it would take. So he donated it to the community college's theater department. It was a good tax break for him."

"It's not like Paul to buy property without thoroughly investigating it, is it?" Jane asked.

Shelley grinned. "That wasn't the real

reason he bought it, I have to admit. But never let him know I told you this. It used to be a movie theater and it was where he saw the first film he ever watched. A black-and-white cowboy epic. He still remembers that as one of his best childhood experiences. The building was due to be leveled to make a parking lot."

"Paul is sentimental?" Jane was astonished.

"Only about a very few things and people. Thank goodness, I'm one of them," Shelley said, coming close to blushing.

"I still don't understand how this theater thing involves us," Jane said warily.

"The college is putting on a play, and we'll cater the food. The rehearsals start at six and go to nine forty-five. Most of the students and teachers involved won't have time to have dinner between their last class of the day and the rehearsal."

Jane frowned. "We're not supposed to cook anything, are we? If so, count me out right now."

"No, it's just snacky stuff for halfway through rehearsals. Sandwiches, chips, soft drinks. On paper plates. I've hired ten different caterers to try out, so it's not always the same kind of food."

"Where on earth did you find ten different caterers?"

"In the phone book. I ignored all the fast-food places that would bring stuff that anybody could drive through to eat. Then I asked twenty of the rest to send me references with the name of the organization and the name and telephone number of the person who'd hired them. Fifteen replied."

Jane should have known that Shelley was well prepared.

"How long does this go on? Ten whole days in a row?" Jane thought it sounded really boring.

"No," Shelley said. "We only do five a week. The students get out of class at noon on Saturday. And they get Sundays off to do all their homework."

"Do we have to hang around? Do we collect all the paper plates and plastic spoons?"

"No, the caterers do that. We merely supervise. And we get to sit in on the rehearsals."

"Why would we want to do that?"

"Because I've run through most of the most expensive caterers around here for Paul's annual dinner for his managers. I want to try out some new ones."

"I meant, why would we want to watch the rehearsals? Eating is fine."

"I thought it might be interesting," Shelley said. "I've never seen anything being rehearsed. Do they change things as they go along? Are there some scenes that look good on paper and just don't work —"

"I don't like amateur theater," Jane interrupted. "We don't have to sit through the whole rehearsal every evening, do we?"

"What's wrong with amateur theater?"

"The actors are — well — amateurs. They always overact. They shout and gesture madly so they can be heard and seen from the back row."

"How do you know this?"

"I took a theater class in college," Jane admitted. "I thought it would be a slam-dunk class I could ace. Instead, I had to attend, and review, every single play and opera the school and local community produced. It was among the most annoying, stupid things I've ever done to myself."

"Don't worry. We don't have to show up early. The snacks are served around eight p.m. We can arrive at seven-thirty. I'd like to watch, though. You could take your laptop and work on your next book in the greenroom, if you'd like."

"My *next* book?"

"Aren't you already thinking about another book?" Shelley asked. "You *will* sell this one, and the publisher will probably want another."

Jane set her fork down and said with chagrin, "You sometimes spook me out, Shelley. I *am* thinking of a next book. I've started making notes about other characters."

There. She'd said it. Out loud. She was going to do this. Now that she'd admitted it to Shelley, she was committed to do so.

"About Priscilla again?"

"No. I've gone as far as I can with Priscilla. I need a new heroine. And I need to make it a mystery from the first, not after I've already written and have to rewrite like I did this time. So, when do these rehearsals start?"

"Not until a week from now. And the building is air-conditioned, in case you were going to ask."

"That's good to know. That saves me from a nasty surprise."

Jane had broken down and bought herself and her younger son Todd new computers the year before. When she was researching background material for the book about Priscilla, she had joined several

Internet listservs that had to do with the time period she was using. That had led her to realize that she might get terribly backlogged if she went out of town, to visit Mike at college or just for the fun of getting away. So she bought a laptop computer as well. She told herself that it would also create a backup if her real computer went haywire or she lost the backup disk. This, she knew deep in her heart, was a silly indulgence. The truth was she thought laptops were cute and handy. Now it would finally be genuinely useful.

She brought it downstairs early the next morning and transferred the notes she'd made about the main character, who was growing in her mind.

She started the first two pots of pasta, and set a timer so she wouldn't forget and cook them to paste or let them burn to the bottom. She started pecking away at the tiny keyboard. Her character had decided on her own name.

Letitia.

The moment it had come to mind, Jane knew it was right. She was setting the next book in the Edwardian era, fifty years or later than the one about Priscilla. Lots of new research to do.

Chapter Two

By the next week, Jane was used to the tiny keyboard and had figured out a rough idea of a plot. She didn't want to spend years on this book, as she had on the first one. Finishing the first in anticipation of attending a mystery conference a few months earlier had taught her a lot.

First, and most important, was learning that she could actually finish a whole book. Second, she needed to know more about the motives, setting, characters, and clues before she started. When she'd started on the book about Priscilla, the name of the main character was really all she knew. It was no wonder it took her so many years to turn it into a novel.

She'd had no "map" that time. Worse, she'd had no list. Jane was an obsessive list maker in every other area of her life. Why hadn't she realized that she needed to apply this skill to writing?

One thing she'd sensed, if not heard precisely, at the mystery conference was that writing was a job. A profession. At least for those who had been successfully published. Even Felicity Roane, her favorite author, had a new book out every nine or ten months. You couldn't do that by winging it every day, Jane suspected.

When she'd started the first book, she'd considered it something that might turn into a book. Or maybe only a fairly long short story. She had had no plan at all.

This time she wanted a map — of sorts. The main things she wanted to see and do if she were to take a long road trip. Conversely, she wanted to be able to wander the side roads when she spotted a billboard that promised there was something interesting to do or eat or learn about if you turned off at the next exit. That would be the best way to approach it if she wanted to succeed in the long run.

She'd already started making notes about who was the perp, who were the other likely suspects — and what their supposed motives were. There was also a list of clues, four or five good ones, she hoped she could insert without drawing attention to them. She was still working on a list of twenty or twenty-five things that might or might not happen.

Unlike her usual lists, which had to be in chronological order and all completed in one day, this could be random and fluid.

Some of her ideas were really off the wall and she didn't know if she'd pursue them. And anything that popped into her mind as she worked could be added.

She'd also decided she should sit in on some of the rehearsals, or at least ask for a copy of the script that would be used for the community theater play. It was, if Shelley was right, a lightweight mystery story set in the 1930s. It might provide some additional insights. If not, it wouldn't matter. She already had a vague sense of what she should be doing.

On the morning of the day Jane and Shelley were due to attend the beginning of the rehearsals that evening, they also took their first lesson in Beginner's Needlepoint. Both of them had admitted to having tried it when they were younger and made a botch of it. The materials cost fifty dollars, but that included a book of patterns, the canvas, needles, and thread. The lessons themselves were ten dollars each and would take place on Tuesday and Thursday mornings for four weeks.

The teacher was a woman in her late fifties, Jane guessed, and the class was held at her needlepoint shop in a room in the back. She had all sorts of her own work displayed and some borrowed from former students, in the shop and in the small classroom.

"We'll start with introductions. I'm Martha Haworth. Call me Martha."

Jane and Shelley introduced themselves as longtime friends and next-door neighbors. A young woman with brutally short blond hair and a bit too much makeup said her name was Tazz. The next student was in her late twenties and very well groomed. *Junior League,* Jane thought. Her name was Elizabeth. Elizabeth didn't say so out loud, but made it clear that calling her Liz wasn't acceptable.

The fifth student was a middle-aged man, with a fierce-looking mustache and old-fashioned sideburns. "I'm Sam. My wife does needlepoint and I'd like to learn, but someone years ago told me not to ever ask someone who calls you 'honey' to instruct you."

Everybody laughed.

"The basics are simple," Martha said as she passed out books. "There are two kinds of needlepoint canvas. Mono, which is one thread, stiffly starched. And penelope, which is double strands very close together. We're starting with mono, which is thirteen holes to the inch. It's the

20

best for using cotton floss. Good coverage, but not too fat. If you prefer to work in wool, we'll cover that later. And I've put together a bag of goodies from the shop for each of you.

"What you're going to do first is a sampler," she went on. "As many different stitches as you'd like to try. They're all in this book." She handed out a seventy-five-page book with detailed instructions on how to stitch sixty different patterns. The rest of it was a few colored pictures of ten of the examples, followed by an index. Martha let them browse through it for a few minutes.

She then distributed equal-sized canvases, all with a lightweight binding around the edge. "I'm going to turn you loose in the shop now. I'd suggest you choose three colors that you like together. I have a color wheel you can consult. I suggest you choose one packet of floss for each color, one in a fairly light tone, and another of a medium tone, and a third a little darker. If you run out, you can always come to the shop for more. You want Number 3 weight cotton floss for this project. There are books on the front counter you can consult for what colors come in what sizes."

Jane hadn't paid a lot of attention to the

shop on the way in and was stunned by the variety of colors available. She chose a combination of pinks, purples, and an off-white called ecru. Shelley picked greens, blues, and yellows.

When they were corralled back in the workroom, they compared their choices. Sam had chosen tans, blues, and ecru. Tazz had picked violent reds, blues, and stark white. Elizabeth had chosen colors that looked awful together to Jane — oranges, greens, and reds. All in sort of muddy hues.

The teacher's last remarks were warnings. "Don't get nervous and stitch too tight. It will buckle the canvas. Don't stint on imagination. Make strips, odd sizes of rectangles or triangles. I'm giving each of you a packet of gridded paper to experiment with. There are also markers if you want to outline your pattern on the canvas. Don't worry, it will disappear when the work is washed. Remember to mark the canvas on the threads, not on the valleys between them.

"Wash your hands well before each session of work," she went on. "All this is in the packet, along with the right size blunt needles, and leather thimbles if you need them. We'll meet again on Thursday at the same time and see how much progress everyone has made. Have fun. And it's not a contest. It's just for fun. Keep that in mind.

"And my final advice is the most important, even though I mentioned it fleetingly already. Just like in knitting, crocheting, and sewing, use a light hand. It will save your fingers and keep the work looking good. If you work too tight, it will hurt you and your project both."

When Jane and Shelley arrived at the theater early that evening, Jane was astonished at the size and faded grandeur of the building. She tried the door, which was locked. "Never mind. I have a key," Shelley said.

The large lobby, which had held up a little better than the outside, was truly grand. Elaborate gold-foiled trim around the two-story-high ceiling. Red marble floors. The same marble for pillars.

Shelley guided them through the large seating area. Jane admired the balconies, but was surprised that there was nobody on the stage. They heard voices and followed them to a room well behind the stage where there was a long table and chairs crammed close together. The backstage part of the theater wasn't nearly as grand as the public spaces. There had apparently been renovations several times. Some of the walls weren't even painted.

Three people were already there, poring over scripts that looked fairly well worn. The young man at the head of the table stood up and said, "You must be Mrs. Nowack and Mrs. Jeffry. I'm Steven Imry. I'm the playwright and the Director." Jane could hear the capital *D* in his voice.

He continued, "I'm a graduate of the theater school at the college. I'm more than halfway through my master's degree, and this is the second full-length play I've directed. Like the students among us who are on the Fast Track program, so are we. That's why we're rehearsing at night from six to ten. You're the ladies who are feeding us, right?"

Jane instinctively didn't like the look of him. He had deep frown lines on his forehead. His sandy hair was thinning. He wore old clothes that were all a little bit too big for him. And worst of all, he was one of those men with a tiny lump of beard just under his lower lip. She always thought this sort of mini-goatee looked like the man had chewed up a dead mouse and couldn't imagine why somebody would make himself look disgusting on purpose.

"So to speak," Shelley said with a hint of hauteur in her voice. "I've arranged for the catering and want to keep an eye on the people I've chosen to do it."

"And you?" he asked, turning to Jane.

"I'm just a taster and observer," she admitted.

She was still considering him. It was more than his appearance that bothered her, though. His voice was too loud. His clothing was shabby and he didn't smell quite clean. It seemed to her that it was a deliberate fashion statement.

Jane and Shelley sat down at the far end of the room. There were two rows of chairs apart from those around the table. Shelley looked at Jane and asked, "What's in that big bag you have? It's not your laptop bag."

Jane reached into the brown canvas bag and pulled out a rolled-up lightweight fabric that was flat and had about forty clear, soft plastic pockets. Many of them were filled with the different colored flosses she'd bought at the needlepoint shop that morning. Each color had a label and a piece of the floss itself tied around it so she could be sure to buy the right color if she needed more. One clear plastic pocket held tiny scissors and one contained four extra needles. Jane was pretty certain she'd lose at least two of them before she was done with this project.

"What a neat thing! I didn't see that in the shop," Shelley said.

"No. It's meant for jewelry. I have one for you, too. A couple of well-meaning people who mistakenly thought I might own lots of jewelry have given them to me over the years. I knew I'd eventually find some other use for them."

Chapter Three

"You're not the only one here, Steve," another man said. Jane and Shelley were both startled and whirled around to where the voice had come from. He'd been sitting behind them. This man was about the same age as the director. He radiated goodwill. He rose from the chair and came around to introduce himself to Jane and Shelley as Jake Stanton.

"But in the play, I'm Edward Weston, the hero's younger brother." He was a bit on the beefy side, but much more attractive than the director. He had a mop of unruly curly brown hair, a charming crooked smile, and good teeth. Jane always noticed people's teeth. Shelley always remembered the color of their eyes. Jane could hardly remember the color of her own eyes.

Steve Imry spoke up. "Jake, I'm glad you introduced yourself by your script name. That's what we're going to do from now on. I've instituted this policy before, and it works well. It makes for a more cohesive cast."

Jake smiled before he turned to go to the

table, and he winked at Jane and Shelley. It was clearly a joke aimed at the pompous director.

The third person had said nothing. She hadn't even taken her eyes from her script.

Jake sat down across the table from her and said to Jane and Shelley, "The sphinx sitting at the far end of the table is, according to our esteemed director, Angeline Smith. The showgirl tramp my big brother is bringing home to meet the parents."

The young woman finally looked up and spoke. "He means my character is a showgirl tramp. My real name is Joani. With an *i* at the end."

She was voluptuous and wore a red, clingy top that looked like the top half of bathing suit specifically designed to show off her impressive cleavage. Her hair was so long and so glossy that Jane supposed it was a wig. Her makeup was a tad on the garish side.

Joani-with-an-i went back to reading her script and Shelley and Jane exchanged a glance. Each knew what the other was thinking.

Everyone was immediately distracted by the entrance of an elderly couple. They stood posed as if they owned the theater and all those who were present. They were obviously waiting for the proper accolades.

"I'm so looking forward to working with you, Gloria and John," the director gushed. "Please make yourselves comfortable. Sit anywhere you'd like. Would either of you like a glass of white wine? I have a bottle chilled."

"Good man," John Bunting croaked. He sat down next to Joani and looked down her cleavage with a leer.

Jane had seen this couple, Gloria and John Bunting, that morning on a local television news show. They both seemed to think they were true stars. The interviewer had obviously never heard of them, and had asked them chirpily what movies they'd been in.

"Movies?" Gloria had drawled in a surprisingly deep voice for such a small woman, "Oh dear, too many to remember. But we started in live theater and have always felt more comfortable with a real audience."

The interviewer asked, to his later regret, what famous plays they'd been in. John rattled off a long, slightly slurred list of productions the interviewer (and Jane) had never heard of.

John Bunting leaned close to Joani and said, "You sure are a looker."

Joani got a whiff of his breath and moved her chair away from him, then turned her back to continue reading her script.

"John," Gloria said, "mind your manners." She tossed one of her many wayward scarves around her throat to make her point. She went around the table and made John sit in another chair, while she sat next to Joani. She slapped her husband's copy of the script in front of him.

Professor Imry said, "I know it's unusual to send scripts out before the first reading session, but we're short on rehearsal time and I wanted the Buntings, in particular, to be prepared. I hope you've all read them and have them pretty well memorized already."

Jane studied Gloria Bunting. She looked better in real life than on television. She was about five foot four, slim but not skinny. She, like most aging actresses, had probably undergone a good deal of plastic surgery. If so, it didn't show. She had a small, thin nose, high cheekbones, and only a hint of wrinkles. Really good shoulders, which didn't seem to be padding. She must have been a very pretty woman when she was younger and was still attractive.

It wasn't easy to guess her age. She could be anywhere from sixty-five to seventy-five.

Her luxuriant white, slightly curly hair looked as if it was her own, not a wig. Her eyes were a clear, perceptive light blue. She moved erectly and easily. No hint of arthritis. Only her hands gave away that she was old. A few age spots. A couple of slightly enlarged knuckles. Jane hoped she'd age as well as Gloria Bunting had.

An extraordinarily good-looking and well-dressed young man had come into the room while Imry finished speaking. He spotted the elderly pair and came over to introduce himself. "I'm Denny Roth," he said, patting them on the shoulders patronizingly. "You've probably heard of me. I've been in several independent films. One of them won several awards at Sundance."

Jake was still sitting near Jane and Shelley and made a small snorting noise and winked at them again. "As an extra, wasn't it, Denny?"

Denny ignored this and took a seat next to the director. Jake introduced Jane and Shelley. "Mrs. Jeffry and Mrs. Nowack are going to make sure that we get fed and watered. Be extra nice to them if you know what's good for you."

Steven Imry clearly didn't like someone else making the rules and introductions.

He stood in front of the head chair and said, "Starting now, we're going to use your characters' names at all times, as I said before. I've —"

Gloria cut him off. "I'm Ms. Gloria Bunting and don't you forget it, young man."

"Gloria is right," her husband agreed. "That's simply not how it works in a *real* theater, Professor. You might wish to be trendy, but it's not professional."

It seemed as if Imry hadn't recognized that he had offended the actress and her husband. Or maybe he didn't care. "It's a technique I've used before with great success. It gets everyone into the spirit of the play sooner. You'll address me as Professor Imry. Tonight is simply a first reading. No gestures, no movements. We'll get to those tomorrow. I just want to hear you emote."

There were a few muttered groans, but Jane couldn't tell who they came from. The older actors simply shook their heads. Shelley muttered almost silently, "Emote?"

Jane had also cringed at the use of "emote." She smiled at Shelley. The longer they'd been friends, the more they thought alike — most of the time. But not always. For instance, they disagreed violently about how books you owned should be treated.

She put this thought aside as the reading started. Jane was surprised at the different ways each actor read. John Bunting, now designated by the director as Mr. Walter Weston, slurred his words, but seemed to have already memorized the script. That surprised her. But on reflection, it shouldn't have. It was probably how he had earned his living from his youth. He looked a great deal older than his wife. He obviously dyed his thinning hair. He'd run to fat and had the bloodshot eyes and the big red nose of a heavy drinker.

His wife, Gloria, who played Mrs. Edina Weston in the script, was letter perfect and didn't even open the script to follow it. She took on a sort of Katharine Hepburn accent when she was speaking.

Joani-with-an-i wasn't nearly as well prepared and had to follow each of her lines with her long-nailed, red-painted forefinger.

Professor Imry was appalled. "You should have had this from memory by now, Angeline. I expect you to have it down by tomorrow's first rehearsal," he warned. "At this stage, you could be replaced."

She nodded sullenly, but her attitude

was a bit fearful as well.

Denny Roth, who had the role of Todd Weston, the handsome, wayward son who had brought Angeline home to his family as his betrothed, had the script memorized by now as well, but read as if he were already bored with it, apparently changing some of Professor Imry's wording.

Imry chastised him. "Read it as if you mean it, and don't improvise."

"It's not my voice the way you've written it. I sound too old. My character's vocabulary and sentence patterns should be his own, not yours."

Jane had just noticed that there were several extra scripts on the table next to her chair at the back of the room. She took one and handed another to Shelley.

Imry's face turned bright red. "This is *my* script. And I'm the director. You will read it the way it's written and is being directed."

"I'm not as easily replaced as Joani, you know," Denny said. "You don't seem to know my character as well as you should. Where did I go to high school? My parents are rich. They'd send me to the best private schools. I'd know better grammar than you've let me use in this script. It's absurd that the script tells me to say 'Angeline and *me* are getting married.' The correct way is 'Angeline and *I* are getting married,' and I'd be well enough educated to know it."

Imry pretended he hadn't heard. "Continue. It's Edward's line next."

Edward, who was really Jake, had it memorized. He played a sort of comic-relief younger brother. Somehow he managed to make Imry's stiff writing light and almost amusing. Jane thought of all of them, he might be the best actor, except for Ms. Bunting.

The next bit of script was spoken by someone Jane hadn't even noticed before. He hadn't been introduced. Glancing at the script, she saw that he had the role of the butler, Cecil, and that his real name was Bill Denk.

"Madam and sir, Cook says luncheon will be served in ten minutes." He was a young man, but spoke in the cracked voice of an elderly retainer.

Jane and Shelley both glanced at their watches. Enduring this wrangling wasn't exactly fun. "Could we slip out now?" Jane whispered.

"Why not. Nobody needs us here," Shelley admitted.

They went outside and Shelley found them a place to sit on a wall in the shade of a small tree. She gestured at the building and said, "Paul found out that this theater has a long and interesting history. At the beginning, this was a pricey neighborhood, and the building was a nice theater with live actors — this was before radio and television. Then the neighborhood started going to pot, several patrons were robbed on the way to their carriages, and another, nicer theater was built elsewhere.

"Over the years," she went on, "it sat vacant for long periods, then was turned into a movie theater. Was closed again. Then a developer bought it and rented it to a church. The church bought two of the small houses next to it to tear down and make parking places."

"How did Paul learn all this?" Jane asked.

"You can hire people who research old papers and do title searches. Anyway, the older people in the church started moving to Florida or dying off, and the church couldn't make the payments, so the building was empty again. For a short while it was used as a soup kitchen. Half the dressing rooms were made into that little kitchen, and the room where they're meeting now was where the people ate. Then for a while groups could rent out the kitchen and eating room for craft groups. And the final use was for A.A. meetings in the audience seating area. In one of the intervals, urban renewal made the neighborhood a lot better."

"Quite an interesting background," Jane said. "Somebody should save that information and post it somewhere in the building. How did it come into Paul's possession?"

"The old guy who'd owned it forever died. His grandchildren didn't want to be responsible for keeping it up, and were going to demolish it and sell the land," Shelley explained. "Paul, as I told you, bought it, and donated it to the college when he realized he couldn't use it for storing food, because it couldn't be brought up to code. So he had it cleaned up, had a few repairs done to the roof and brickwork, and donated it to the college."

"So he managed to save it. That was good of him."

"I'm sort of sorry I dragged us into this," Shelley admitted. "Let's make a deal here. We're not part of the cast. We can call the actors by their real names, okay?"

Jane sighed with relief. "That was going to be my suggestion, too. I'm not good at remembering names anyway, and especially not two sets of names for the same person. I'm curious as to why these rehearsals aren't done during the day."

"It's because the students are on what's called Fast Track Summer, which means they can do a whole semester's work in seven weeks. But they have to take every class every day, with one-hour breaks for studying for exams. That's why they can't get here until six."

"Oh, yes. Imry said something like that but I wasn't paying enough attention."

"That's an interesting concept. I'm going to ask Mike if his college does that."

"I'm going to hide this script in my briefcase and take it home to read tonight," Shelley said. "So far I'm not much impressed with it."

"I don't like the director," Jane said. "I think it's unfortunate he's also the writer of the script. Too much ego bundled in one person. It's odd about the casting, don't you think?"

"In what way?" Shelley asked.

"With the proper makeup and clothing, the Weston family will look like they're all related. Imry did make good choices in this case."

"You think so?" Shelley was perplexed. "They don't even have the same colored eyes. Both the Buntings are blue eyed, and the older son's eyes are brown. That's impossible, I think."

"Shelley, we see them up close. The audience won't see the color of their eyes. I wasn't crazy, I have to admit, about Denny."

"What's wrong with Denny? He was right about his character's background and was dead on about 'Angeline and me.' "

"But it was wrong of Denny to tackle him that way in front of all of us. He should have taken Imry aside and told him that his grammar was wrong in private instead of showing off in front of all of us. I think I'm having heatstroke," Jane said, sorry that she'd brought up the subject of casting. She stood up. "We don't have to sit out here in the heat any longer, do we?"

"I just dragged you out here to air a few opinions. Since we agree, we can wait inside." Shelley glanced at her watch. "The caterer will be parking the van in the back alley any minute now."

Chapter Four

While Shelley was letting the caterers in through the back of the theater and showing them where to prepare and serve the snack supper, Jane took out the canvas bag she'd brought along and removed her needlepoint project. She'd been working on it all day. Looking at the patterns in the book she'd been given, she realized quickly that most of them, except the bargellos, were in sets of four or six stitches. She'd roughed out a basic pattern that could accommodate either multiples of four or multiples of six.

She'd only done two patterns so far. One was a square block of jacquard in light and dark blue in the upper left corner. The pattern beneath it was a cashmere diagonal in a long strip down the left side in a dark pink and dark purple. She was contemplating which colors and patterns to do next when Gloria Bunting, who had no dialogue in the scene they were reading through, walked over and sat down beside Jane.

"That's lovely," she said. "I was a friend of the actress Sylvia Sidney and she was always needlepointing on the set. She did lovely work. I envied the skill. She showed me the basic stitches, but I didn't follow through."

Jane smiled. "You know she did at least one instructional book about needlepoint, don't you? I have a copy at home. I bought it when I tried this years ago and failed. Now Shelley and I are taking lessons."

"When are the lessons? And are they close by?"

"The first was this morning. There are two sessions a week, one each Tuesday and Thursday morning for four weeks, right here in town. The woman limits the class to five. But maybe she'd be willing to add a celebrity."

Gloria was pleased at this description. "Could I catch up tomorrow? Maybe you could take me to the shop and tell me what I need to buy. Although I think I should start something smaller than what you're working on. The arthritis in my hands might make it impossible."

"Are you going to be here long enough to take the whole course?"

"Good Lord, I hope so. We contracted for two weeks of rehearsals and three weeks of performances. I don't think this dog of a play will last that long, but I'd stay over to finish the course anyway if it doesn't."

Jane reached in her canvas bag and showed Gloria the instruction book. "It's fifty dollars for the bound canvas, this book, the needles, and enough thread to make something this size. I think that's a bargain. Then the lessons are ten dollars for two hours of help and advice. At least you'd have all the information to take along when the play is done."

"I need something to do while I'm here. We don't normally do these amateur things in which all the rehearsals are in the evenings. I like to put in almost a full day's work, then relax at night until the play starts. This is the opposite. This time we're working at night and I need something to fill the mornings. Of course, both John and I grew up here and now our daughter lives here, too. So we have grandchildren to visit with on weekend mornings."

Shelley reappeared from the next room and said, "The snack supper is ready. I hope it's a good time for a short break. You're welcome to fill your plates and bring your food back in here, if you like."

"Excuse me, Ms. Nowack?" Imry said. "I don't remember carrying around food being part of the arrangement."

Shelley stared at him for a long moment and said, "This is a charitable donation. You do remember that, don't you? And there is a handy old phrase that 'beggars can't be choosers.' Besides, I arranged it this way so you wouldn't lose rehearsal time."

"But it was a rude way to state it," Imry said.

"And who started the rudeness?" Shelley asked.

Bill Denk, who played the butler, grinned at Shelley, saying in his old-man voice, "You go, girl," and started clapping. It was taken up by the others.

Imry rose, red-faced, and went into the next room ahead of everyone else.

"Jane," Shelley said, "we have to nibble a bit of everything to note the taste and texture and such of the food. I know we've both eaten dinner, but I'd appreciate it if you would —"

She came to a dead halt, staring at Jane's needlepoint canvas. "You've already started?"

"Of course I have," Jane said. "I planned it on the computer this afternoon. I bought Todd a grid program when he was working on those prime numbers, don't you remember?"

"While I was making out my detailed checklist to fill out on the caterers?" Shelley asked in a wounded voice. "I thought we'd be working together. Oh well, I guess that really isn't practical."

Jane told Shelley, "Ms. Bunting would like to go to the needlepoint shop with us in the morning and catch up with what we did today. Don't you think — since Ms. Bunting is so famous and actually knew Sylvia Sidney — that the teacher would take one more person?"

Shelley turned to Gloria Bunting. "You really *knew* Sylvia Sidney?" she exclaimed, her annoyance with Jane forgotten. "I love her movies."

"She was as wonderful in real life," Ms. Bunting said. "What is that thing you're keeping your yarn in, Ms. Jeffry?"

"It's supposed to be for jewelry. But the individual pockets are great for keeping the colors from being in a jumble. We could shop for one for you tomorrow."

"That's so kind of you. We have a rental car. I could drive."

"It would be easier if I drive," Jane said. There was no way she was letting Shelley scare an old woman to death with her driving. Nor did she trust that Ms. Bunting would get them where they were going.

She might be an even worse driver than Shelley.

The three of them went into the other room. Gloria Bunting took little dabs of everything, as Jane and Shelley had done. The rest piled their paper plates high. Shelley gave this caterer good marks for providing sturdy paper plates, plastic silverware that looked better than most, and delivering a few hot dishes instead of merely cold pasta salads, cold bread, and deli-type meats. The bread received her highest mark. Not only was it warm, it was already buttered with real butter (or something that tasted like real butter). It was crusty and had caraway seeds on the outside that still tasted good. Shelley felt strongly that the spices caterers used should be fresh.

Jane and most of the cast took their food out to the big table in the other room. Shelley wanted to stay in the room with the caterers to watch how they worked. Professor Imry stayed there to eat as well, making his point that this was what he'd expected.

"The caterers will clean that table where the rest are eating, won't they?" he asked Shelley haughtily.

Before she could reply, the owner of the

company said, "Mrs. Nowack, that wasn't in the contract, but for *you,* we'll do so."

"That's gracious, William. Thanks."

Shelley gave Imry another critical look, which he pretended to ignore, but he got red in the face again.

Shelley stayed in the serving area of the theater to watch the cleanup. These caterers were efficient. They brought along their own bags to take away the trash, and they cleaned every surface they'd used, including the floor. They asked everyone to pick up their scripts so they could clean the big table in the room where most of the cast had eaten. As Shelley stashed her critique in her briefcase and Jane rolled up her needlepoint and put it in her canvas bag, Ms. Bunting gave Jane a slip of paper.

"This is where we're staying. The telephone number is for our suite. Let me know if and when we can go to the needlepoint shop."

"I think they open at ten in the morning," Jane said. "The owner will probably be in by at least nine forty-five. I'll call and tell her we'd like to bring you. If you don't mind, I'll use your connection with Sylvia Sidney to impress her."

"I wouldn't mind at all. I'm so glad to have met you girls."

When they were in Jane's car, Shelley said, "I haven't been referred to as a 'girl' in ages. What a sweet woman Ms. Bunting is."

When Jane called Martha the next morning at eight-thirty, she was glad the proprietor was already at work. Jane's mention of the extra student went over well. Martha had even heard of Gloria Bunting. She'd seen her in Connecticut in the out-of-town first performance of a play that was going to New York a month later. "She played a sort Mrs. Danvers–like role. She was wonderfully wicked."

When Jane told Martha that Ms. Bunting had been a friend of Sylvia Sidney, the woman nearly swooned. "I'd be delighted to add her. Bring her along as soon as you like. She won't even have to pay for the lessons, only the materials. I'm so thrilled about this. I can't wait to meet her in person."

Jane called Shelley first. "We're all set. I'll call Ms. Bunting and tell her to be ready to be picked up at a quarter to ten. I'll drive. We also need to figure out where to get her one of these jewelry things for her floss."

"I'm glad you're driving. I need to call

the caterers for tonight and tell them there will be four more people. Two doing scenery, another doing props, and one responsible for costumes."

Ms. Bunting was thrilled to hear from Jane. "John's gone off with cronies from the old days to play golf. They'll probably all collapse from heatstroke. I'll be in front of the hotel waiting for you — just roll down a window and wave at me. I'm so glad you made these arrangements! I'd have been bored senseless and worrying about John's health if you hadn't."

Shelley made her call to the caterer. She also called several department stores that had good jewelry departments to see if any of them had one of those roll-up jewelry things with the clear pockets. She found one place that did.

"It's in that mall across from where we stayed for the mystery conference. We could take Ms. Bunting to lunch at that fabulous restaurant we discovered there, after we get her all set up."

"You like her, don't you? So do I," Jane said.

Martha at the needlepoint shop was gracious to Ms. Bunting, but had calmed down and didn't gush too effusively — except for wanting to know which play she had been in with Sylvia Sidney. Ms. Bunting said it was *Summer Wishes, Winter Dreams* in 1973. Sylvia was one of the leads. Ms. Bunting was offered only a small part, but she took it in order to get to know Sylvia. "She was almost as old then as I am now. But she had more energy than I do. You know, she was once married to the publisher Bennett Cerf, and again to an actor named Luther Adler. She only died in 1999. She was eighty-nine years old. A very durable woman."

"Indeed she was. And I've heard of both of her husbands," Martha said. "Well, I shouldn't take more of your time with this just now. I want to get you set up for class tomorrow."

Ms. Bunting chose a combination of mauves, slate blues, and several clear greens. Martha told her what the assignment was, adding, "But you, of course, Ms. Bunting, may do anything you wish."

Chapter Five

Jane dropped Shelley and Ms. Bunting at one of the entrances to the mall, then parked, as she always did, as far away as she could so that nobody was near enough to her car to ding it. In her eagerness to rejoin her friends, Jane trotted back to the entrance, arriving breathless and a bit sweaty.

"We've found something you'll like," Shelley told Ms. Bunting. "Would you like to come up the escalator with us to fetch it, or would you rather take a table and save it for us in our favorite restaurant? The restaurant is much closer. And you could order our drinks while we're gone."

"The second option sounds best to me. I'm absolutely parched," the older woman admitted. "I wasn't expecting all this heat."

They made sure they settled her by a window, and headed upstairs to buy the jewelry container for her flosses. Shelley slapped down a credit card and they rushed back down to the ground floor as soon as the clerk produced the receipt.

Ms. Bunting was already settled in, with

a bottle of white wine for herself and Shelley, and the rose-flavored iced tea that Jane had requested.

Shelley reached into the department store bag and brought out the jewelry container, which was almost identical to the ones she and Jane had.

"Oh!" Ms. Bunting exclaimed. "How dear of you pretty girls to get this. You must let me reimburse you."

"No, it's a gift. We're all too hungry to mess around with money right now," Shelley proclaimed. "Besides, Jane and I wanted you to have it as a gift."

"Then I'll pay for our lunch," Ms. Bunting said.

"Let's just be nuisances and ask for separate checks and you and Shelley can split the cost of the wine," Jane suggested.

They all agreed that this was fair. They studied the extensive menu and all chose different salads and entrées to share around.

"Would you like for me to go back to the car and get your flosses and needles while you two place our order?" Jane asked Ms. Bunting.

"I can't let you do that. It's too hot out there. Besides, it will give me something fun to do at leisure when I'm back at my hotel," the older woman said.

They fell to gossiping about the cast, and agreed wholeheartedly that the most annoying by far was the director. Ms. Bunting said, "John and I seldom do amateur productions like this. It was only because we have family and friends here. I hadn't even looked at the script until we were on the plane, and was shocked at how silly it is."

"Shelley and I purloined two scripts yesterday," Jane said, "and glanced over them. We agreed that it's obvious he's never even read a mystery. The reader or viewer deserves to know whodunit and why at the end. And he has no sense of humor. Are you sure you can't back out?"

"An actor *never* backs out," Ms. Bunting exclaimed. "No matter how bad the script is, we'll bring what talent we still possess to it. We'll just warn our local friends not to attend, as it's a miserable script."

They didn't get any further with their criticisms because the salads arrived. All three were gigantic. "I'll never get through this and the pasta dish I ordered," Ms. Bunting said.

"They're used to guests like us. They'll box it up for us to take home," Jane reassured her.

At the end of the meal, Ms. Bunting was

looking tired. "I'm seldom up as early as I was today, except on film shoots. They often start at dawn if they're shooting outside scenes, in order to get all the natural light they can."

"We'll take you right straight back to your hotel for a nap. I may take one, too," Jane said. "This heat is exhausting."

As they walked her to the hotel entrance, Jane asked, "Would you like Shelley to take your things up to your room for you?"

"No, thanks. I'm not so tired that I can't carry these treasures, not to mention my leftover lunch. See you tonight — and thank you for the lovely day."

"She was really fading away," Jane said as she squeezed her way back into traffic.

"I wonder how old she really is?" Shelley asked.

"I don't think we'll find out. The older the actress, the younger she says she is," Jane replied.

"Not anymore. Jane Fonda, Cher, Sally Field, and a lot of others are bragging about passing fifty these days."

Jane said, "But they all still look thirty-eight. Times and plastic surgery have changed our perception of age since Gloria Bunting's heyday. If there ever really was one for her."

"What do you mean by that?" Shelley asked.

"I saw them on a local morning news show," Jane explained. "The interviewer queried them about what movies they'd made, and both of them turned up their noses at films and said they preferred live theater. They listed a whole lot of plays that they'd been in. Neither the interviewer nor I had ever heard of any of them."

"But you've admitted already that you don't like live acting. And maybe those plays were never made into movies," Shelley said.

"No, I don't like live *amateur* acting. Come to think of it, though, I do prefer movies, especially when I can buy or rent them and fast-forward or stop them when the spaghetti water starts boiling over."

"So we're guessing that Gloria and John Bunting are a sort of third-rate Jessica Tandy and Hume Cronyn," Shelley said with the slightest hint of criticism of Jane's opinion.

"That's not as bad it as it sounds," Jane explained. "Lots of people in any field of the arts can probably eke out a good living doing first-rate work and not gaining enormous fame from it. It's certainly true of writers. I've read a lot of good books by writers who aren't famous, and probably aren't rich, but who tell a good story. It's probably true of actors and artists as well. They make their own niche and fill it."

"I suppose that's right," Shelley said.

"So who are the caterers tonight?" Jane asked.

"An outfit calling themselves 'The Ultimate Meal.'"

"Do you think it will be?"

"At least it's a better name than 'The Ultimate Snack.'"

The rehearsal that evening was a brief walk-through. The main purpose seemed to be to work out details of the play with the two young volunteer art school students who were preparing the single background set, the professional prop master (who was probably being paid), and the costumer (also paid, Jane and Shelley speculated), who needed to measure the actors. Apparently lighting would come later.

"And maybe a sound person to mike the actors," Shelley commented idly.

"I thought real actors had to have the voices to project without a mike?" Jane asked Shelley.

"I guess so, at least this time. If it was something like a musical review, I imagine they would need microphones."

Jane grinned. "Thank goodness that we don't have to learn all about this. All you and I need to consider is food."

As the actors were walking through the first scene again, Bill Denk said, "Madam and sir, Cook says luncheon will be ready at one o'clock."

"I asked her to be ready at quarter to one," Ms. Bunting said in the haughty voice of Mrs. Edina Weston.

"I'll remind her, madam," he said and turned briefly to the audience and said, "The old trout."

"What did you say?" Imry asked.

"Said? Nothing," Bill said.

Jane thought it was funny but also a bit spooky that Bill Denk could cast his voice to the audience but not be heard on stage.

There was no need for Jane and Shelley to be introduced to the newcomers, but they were surprised to see one familiar figure. It was Tazz from the needlepoint lesson they'd taken the day before.

Tazz greeted them after putting a dress bag over an adjoining chair with great care. "I didn't expect to run into you two here," she said with a smile as she sat down in the back row of the theater, where Jane and

Shelley had taken refuge until the caterers arrived.

"Nor did we expect you," Jane said with pleasure.

"We're here to test out caterers for my husband's business dinners," Shelley explained. "They're just making snack suppers for the cast and crew. And you, Tazz? What's your role here?"

"I do the costumes for most of the local productions, and a few costume parties. Mostly around Halloween."

"How did you happen into such an interesting job?" Jane asked.

"I was studying accounting, and decided I'd probably slit my throat from sheer boredom if I had to be an accountant. So, since I'd always sewed my own clothes, I started sewing for other people. Word got around that I was good at period stuff. So — here I am."

"Do you make all the costumes for every play and party?" Shelley asked.

"No. Only special things I don't already have warehoused. When I can, I build in extra hem room, and bosom room in the women's clothes in particular. Sometimes I rent from other costume places if something is too elaborate to use often."

"I just *love* hearing about other people's

jobs," Jane exclaimed. "I've never met anyone who does what you do. I'll bet you have good stories. Sometime when we're all free of this job, I hope you'll have more time to tell us about your experiences."

"I'd be glad to. Now I need to snag everyone for measurements. I guess I'll see you two at tomorrow's needlepoint class."

"Yes, and Ms. Bunting is joining us as well."

"I thought the class was limited to five students," Tazz replied.

"We got her in because she was once in a play with Sylvia Sidney," Jane explained.

"Oh, that makes sense. I have a copy of Sylvia Sidney's needlepoint book," Tazz said. "I'd love to hear what she was really like, aside from acting and needle-pointing."

"I probably have the same book," Jane said. "Did she do more than one?"

"I have no idea," Tazz said.

"I'm sure we would all like to hear what Ms. Bunting knows about her," Shelley agreed. "What's in the dress bag?"

"Ms. Bunting's dress for the first act. I already met with her at her hotel, and it was easy to size her up without taking all the measurements. Later, we'll try it on and get the director's approval. And he *better* approve it. It's going to look grand on her."

As she spoke, Bill Denk, using his old-man voice, returned to the stage. "Madam, Cook says she will have luncheon ready at a quarter before one."

"Of course she will. That was what she was told," Ms. Bunting, as Edina Weston, replied.

"Bossy broad could have thanked me," he said to the theater.

Again, Imry questioned him. "Did you say something not in the script?"

Denk shrugged. "I don't think so."

"All right. I'll play along," Professor Imry said condescendingly. "But don't you try to get away with snide asides when we do this play for a real audience."

Bill just smiled.

Jane nudged Shelley and said quietly, "He's the only thing that might save this awful play."

Shelley nodded. "I wonder how he does it? I've never seen anyone who could throw his voice so well."

"And we both know he's going to keep doing it," Jane said.

Chapter Six

Tazz asked Jane to keep an eye on the dress bag and walked up on the stage. "Forgive me for the interruption, Professor Imry, but I'm the costumer, Tazz Tinker, and I have things I need to tell the cast. Are they all here?"

"We're missing a few still. Denny's not here yet. And the prop person will be fifteen minutes late."

"I don't need to dress the prop person."

Imry gave an embarrassed fake laugh.

"Okay, listen up, actors," Tazz went on, "I'll be measuring all but Ms. Bunting today. I've already found two dresses for her, providing the director agrees. When the measuring is done, I'll find the right size and period clothing for day wear and formal evening wear for the last scene. When each costume is ready to be worn, it will be signed for by the actor who wears it. You will all wear underarm shields that I provide for free. Both perspiration and deodorant are the worst enemies of fabric. If you sweat on the fabric or get makeup on the collar, you will be asked to get it dry-cleaned. If I rent it from a supplier, the college will pay for cleaning and laundry. If it belongs to me, it will be at your own cost. If the stain process doesn't work, you pay for the garment."

"I don't think this is the usual way costumers deal with cast clothing," Imry claimed.

"It's the way *I* work. Take it or leave it," Tazz said. "If you'd done your homework, you'd have known my conditions of providing costumes. I sent you a copy of my rules and you signed them. Now, Professor Imry, I read an early version of the script and didn't notice a police officer as a member of the cast. Has that been fixed?"

"No. The script doesn't call for one."

Tazz looked at him with raised eyebrows. "This is a murder mystery script. In it the butler kills the younger son. You don't need a police presence?"

"That's assumed to take place after the play is over," Imry said, clearly uncomfortable with her question.

Tazz turned to Jane and Shelley, who had brought along the dress bag and were now sitting in the first row of audience chairs, stage left. Tazz rolled her eyes at them, then turned to Imry. "I see," she said in a flat, calm voice. "I'll measure the male actors first, since there are only the maid and Joani I need to get sizes for. Ms. Bunting's costumes are already fitted. Now tell me your real names so I can draw up the contracts."

"We're using the actors' stage names," Imry said.

"I don't contract with fictional characters," Tazz said with a loud laugh. "Now, I recognize Mr. Bunting. Tell me who the other men are."

Imry was forced to forgo his rule. He introduced all the actors by their real names.

"And the man standing just off stage?" Tazz asked. "Is he a backstage worker?"

"No. He's just here to observe."

Jane whispered to Shelley, "Maybe he's a reporter and Imry doesn't want anyone to know it."

"He's not taking notes," Shelley replied.

"Maybe he has a tape recorder in his pocket," Jane responded. "Or . . ."

"Or what?"

"Never mind. It was a silly idea. If I turn out to be right, I'll tell you what it was."

Just then, Denny arrived, flustered. "I had an exam that ran late. That's why I couldn't get here till now. I'm sure I aced it."

The first walk-through rehearsal went

well, as far as Jane and Shelley could tell, except for Bill Denk's improvising. There were no breaks, and the first two acts were done by the time the caterers arrived.

Tazz, who had clearly taken a strong dislike to Imry, sat at the table questioning him as they ate. "So there isn't a police officer. When I read the script, there wasn't any explanation of why the butler murdered the younger son, either."

"That's for the audience to decide for themselves," Imry said smugly.

"Oh, like sophisticated artsy novels that leave the ending unresolved? That's plain lazy writing and too pretentious for the likes of me. I hate books like that," Tazz commented as she wolfed down her snack dinner. She appeared to be anxious to get on with the measuring.

"I read a book like that recently," Ms. Bunting chimed in. Her nap seemed to have completely revived her. "I threw it in the trash."

"Did you throw my script in the trash, too?" Imry asked, obviously looking for an argument.

"I know which side my bread is buttered on," Ms. Bunting said with a wicked smile. "I simply memorized it. That's my job."

"I don't read many books," Joani put

into the conversation, looking around for someone to express admiration of her view. Everybody ignored her.

"This is good food, ladies," Jake, who played the younger son, said to Jane and Shelley, apparently eager to start a harmless discussion.

Both the first two caterers had made sure to provide for hungry vegetarians, which Shelley was pleased to note in her files. The caterer last night had provided raw vegetables with several dipping sauces. Tonight the vegetables were lightly sautéed and served in one large bowl with a heating element under it. The dressing was a bit bland and could have used a good dose of fresh pepper, Jane whispered to Shelley.

Tazz took her empty plate and glass back to the catering room and lurked until John Bunting had finished eating. She snatched his plate to return as well and said, "Come on, Mr. Bunting. I need to measure you."

He leered at her.

Jane sat down with Ms. Bunting. "Tazz is one of the people in the needlepoint class. You'll see her again tomorrow morning."

"She's a strong-minded girl. I'll be curious to see what kind of sampler she's doing."

"Have you started yours yet?" Jane asked.

"Barely. I had such fun putting those pretty colors in the jewelry thing you girls bought me. I'll treasure it forever. I've done only one square. I'm sticking with simple squares for my first effort."

Tazz gathered all the men in one large dressing room. "We're not having any witty remarks about inseams or dressing left or right. Got it? Just tell me the size of your trousers and jackets. I will measure across your shoulders and get the correct arm length. You'll all wear casual trousers circa 1930, shirts, and either jackets or sweaters for the first two acts. The third act will be formal wear. White starched shirts, white formal jackets, black trousers with a silk stripe down the sides."

She finished this process quickly and efficiently, noting all the measurements in a notebook she carried.

Then she cornered Ms. Bunting to try on both of the dresses Tazz had selected for her. Holding the dress bag, Jane was present as well. The everyday one for the first two acts was a drop-waisted pink silk dress with a long string of fake pearls. It had three-quarter-length sleeves. "Other jewelry will be decided on later," Tazz told the actress.

Tazz then called in Imry to approve it. He even managed to eke out a compliment for Tazz on how well it suited the actress and the play.

"The formal dress will be along the same lines, but with black sequins. Don't dare let anyone who smokes near you, Ms. Bunting," Tazz warned, "or the sequins might catch fire — they're notoriously flammable. Even though the sequined one is supposed to have been sprayed with a fire retardant. I haven't chosen jewelry because I don't think it's needed. Just wear your own wedding ring and maybe a pair of smooth silver bracelets."

"You look like a queen," Jane said.

"I feel like one," Ms. Bunting said, pirouetting in front of the three-sided mirror in her dressing room. The skirt flared nicely. "I'll have to find an occasion to do this, just to show off."

"I don't think the director will object to this," Tazz said. "We won't bother getting his approval of this one."

The next morning, Jane called Ms. Bunting at her hotel and offered to pick her up and take her to the needlepoint class.

"It's sweet of you to ask, but I have some shopping to do first, so I'll just take a cab. I have the owner's card with the address in my needlepoint bag. I'll see you then."

Ms. Bunting was only a few moments late. She had a bag from a toy store. "For my grandchildren," she said. As she set the bag down, soft baby toys tumbled out. Jane bent over to pick them up and put them back.

Martha introduced Ms. Bunting to the others, explaining that she, Martha, had bent the rules because Ms. Bunting was a famous actress who had known Sylvia Sidney, who was not only an actress but had written a very good needlepoint book.

Tazz said, "Ms. Bunting and I have met before. I'm providing her costumes for the play she's going to be in in another week, right here in Chicago."

Both Jane and Martha had brought along their copies of Sylvia Sidney's book. Everyone, even those who had never heard of Sylvia Sidney, passed it around and asked questions about her.

Then they all pulled out their needlepoint work to show how they were coming along so far. Tazz's was the most complex. She'd done half of an American flag in the center, which would be surrounded by borders of stars and stripes in different stitches. They were all marked out on the canvas, and she had the kinds of stitches she was using on grid paper.

Ms. Bunting had barely started, but she'd used the upper left corner to do a section of bargello stitches in the darkest shades of each of her three colors and said she intended to do the same stitch in the opposite corner with the lightest shades of the same three colors.

Sam's consisted of fairly boring colors, and he'd stitched a little too tight, but he'd tackled some very complex stitches. "Don't worry," he assured the rest of them. "I know the first ones I did need to be ripped out."

Shelley had tried to catch up with Jane and had done an elongated cashmere stitch with her medium colors.

What most surprised Jane was that Elizabeth's looked the best, in spite of the muddy oranges, greens, and reds. She was way ahead of everyone else. She'd completed nearly a quarter of her project and used what looked like the most difficult stitches in the pattern book. There was an impressive Scotch plaid rectangle, which adjoined a long thin triangle of French knots.

Jane smiled at Elizabeth, who was, in this case at least, every bit as competitive as Shelley.

Chapter Seven

Elizabeth turned out to be rather tactless, in spite of her seemingly upper-crust façade.

After everyone had oohed and aahed over one another's work, Elizabeth said to Ms. Bunting, "Those cute toys must be for your great-grandchildren."

"No. They're for my daughter's children."

"My goodness. She must have had them quite late in life."

Ignoring the obvious suggestion that Ms. Bunting must be at least in her nineties, Ms. Bunting said, "No, it was *I* who had my daughter late in life. I'd always wanted children, but suffered three miscarriages early in our marriage. I'd given up ever having children. Then, when I was forty-two, and doing a very silly movie in England, I found myself pregnant again. It was the worst movie I was ever in, but I was taking such good care of myself that I wasn't paying attention to what was going on around me."

She continued, "John, of course, was deeply embarrassed at becoming a father at forty-three. I don't think, frankly, that he'd have enjoyed the role at any age."

"So, was your daughter born in England?" Elizabeth persisted.

"Unfortunately not. She was born on the ship on the way home. I was afraid to fly. By the time the terrible, endless film was done, I was seven and a half months along."

"It must have been hard, raising a baby at that age. Did you keep acting?" Elizabeth asked.

"I had to. It was the only skill I had," Ms. Bunting said, picking out colors for her next sampler block. "Besides, John and I earned our living acting together. I took along a day nanny and a night nanny, then later both nannies and a teacher. It was very expensive and we had to work even harder to afford the help. I came as close as this," she said, holding her forefinger and her thumb a half inch apart, "to having a nervous breakdown once."

Ms. Bunting abruptly changed the subject. "I think these colors will go well together. Do you agree?" She was holding up three skeins — two light and one medium colors.

Jane leaped in and asked, "What would it look like if you used the darkest instead of the medium?"

This was enough to cut off any more personal questions from Elizabeth. Jane thought it was about time Elizabeth's snoopiness was squelched.

The conversations shifted back to color and pattern choices, with Martha as busy as a hen advising various students. It drifted off into recipes for a bit, then to having pillows made of their work when it was done or having them mounted in acid-free paper and double glass, front and back.

An hour later, packing-up commenced. Ms. Bunting was spending the afternoon with her grandchildren to give them their toys. Elizabeth asked Jane, Shelley, and Ms. Bunting where they had found the wonderful jewelry bags in which they kept their floss, scissors, and needles. Shelley explained about the department store and that they were meant for jewelry.

Jane and Shelley were going home, Shelley intending to get ahead of Jane in the needlepoint ranks.

Jane planned to work on her second book.

Elizabeth, not surprisingly, was headed to a Junior League planning committee.

Tazz was on her way to her warehouse to find the right size costumes.

Sam had to pick up his truck from the garage where he had left it to have the tires rotated while he was in class. He asked Martha if she had a paper bag without the needlepoint shop logo he could put his things in. He didn't want the mechanics to see what he had along.

When Jane returned home, she decided she had to monitor her time. She'd have to put in two hours on her book for each hour of working on her needlepoint. Over a ham sandwich and Fritos, she made notes of what Letitia would be doing next. Then she'd do at least half a chapter and still have time to do a bit of needlepoint before dressing to go out with Mel at five to his favorite steakhouse restaurant. Detective Mel VanDyne and Jane had been friends and lovers for a long time.

But shortly after noon, Mel called. "I'm going to have to stand you up. I've got a murder victim at a theater."

Jane asked warily, "What theater?"

"Why does it matter?"

"It just does."

"It's that one that belongs to the college drama department."

"Who's dead?"

"Jane, I don't even know that yet. I'm still five blocks away. You might want to let

Shelley know. Isn't that the building her husband donated to the college?"

When he hung up, she immediately rang Shelley. "You're going to have to cancel the caterers this minute. I just heard from Mel that someone's been murdered at the theater."

"Who?"

"Even Mel doesn't know yet."

"I'm hanging up and calling the caterer right now. Thanks for letting me know."

Jane's afternoon was shot. She couldn't keep her mind on her book or her needlepoint and sat down to watch the Home and Garden channel to clear her head of this news. She couldn't, however, help speculating about the identity of the victim. Her best guess was Professor Imry. He'd made enemies of almost everyone involved.

He'd mildly insulted Shelley, and he'd irritated both John and Gloria Bunting with his silly insistence on calling actors by their script names at all times. He'd come out on the wrong side of a tiff with Denny Roth about grammar. But who would kill him for getting his grammar wrong? That wasn't even close to being a motive for something so horrible.

And what if it wasn't Imry? Who else

could it be? And how was Mel certain it was murder when he hadn't even reached the scene yet? Maybe someone had just had a terrible accident. A fall. A stroke. A heart attack.

She turned the television off, suddenly horrified that it might be Gloria Bunting who was the victim. It would break Jane's heart if it was. She would also be sad if it was Tazz.

The phone rang again. This time it was Shelley. "I caught the caterers before they'd started the preparations, so all I've lost is my deposit. This is clearly going to close the theater for at least a day, maybe longer. Do you think I should warn the next one in line?"

"I would if I were you."

"Have you heard back from Mel? Who was murdered? Was it really murder or was it an accident?"

"I don't know anything else. But I've also wondered as well."

"Couldn't you call Mel on his cell phone and ask?"

"That would be worth more than my life is. He'd be furious. Call your other caterer, then let's rent a movie and order a take-out dinner for the two of us and our kids."

"Sounds like a good plan. But we'll have

to make sure to catch the local newscasts. Maybe some reporter knows more than we do."

Mel had the whole staff working. The scene-of-the-crime people had quartered the dressing room where the body was found. The doctor had been there to pronounce formally that the victim was dead of causes unknown, but presumably from a blow to the back of his skull. The photos had all been taken and the body moved to the police morgue.

Professor Imry had turned up at two in the afternoon and had been having mild hysterics and demanding to see the officer in charge the whole time.

With everything being competently done on the ground floor, or at least in progress, Mel finally took the time for a preliminary interview with the director. He met with him in the lobby.

"Mr. Imry —" he began.

"*Professor* Imry, if you don't mind. You wouldn't let me call you Mister, would you?"

Mel's first thought was that Imry was right. His second was that his own title was harder to come by and far grittier than Imry's, but he didn't let his annoyance show.

"Professor Imry, how many people have keys to the theater?"

"Why do you ask? Nearly everyone, obviously. Actors are artists and sometimes want to work alone on the stage trying out movements, or how many strides it takes to move where they need to be."

Mel wanted to smack some sense into this man. This was a serious security violation. The college that owned the theater would be horrified if they knew.

"So all the actors had keys? Who else?"

"The janitor. I don't think the costumer needed a key. Let's see, who else? The lighting director had a key — he was going to work with his two students in a dark setting one evening. The electrician — he had to make sure that all the connections were functioning properly. The woman from the art department had one."

"The art department?" Mel asked.

"For the use of the students who were going to build and paint scenery backdrops. Nobody in their street clothes wants to run into wet paint, you see?"

"So nearly everyone and his mother could have come in here at any time?"

"I wouldn't have put it quite that way," Imry said, clearly offended.

"Did you take into consideration the

matter of safety? Did you get approval from the college to give out all these duplicate keys?"

"I didn't think it was necessary. Who could have imagined this sort of thing was going to happen?"

Mel asked for a list of people who had keys, and their telephone numbers and addresses. "I'll have one of my officers call everyone in to get their fingerprints. That can be done in the lobby." He also asked if Imry knew the victim's next of kin. It was vital to reach them.

"I don't have that information, but the registrar of the college will. I think the telephone number is in my office. I'll get it."

"No, you won't. Tell me where your office is and I'll find it. You're not to go anywhere but the lobby for now."

Mel then asked, "Where were you last night after the rehearsal?"

"I went home to do some work on my next script," Imry answered warily.

"Can anybody back you up on this?"

"Maybe someone in the apartment complex where I live noticed me come in or took note that my car was parked in my assigned place."

"Give me your address."

Imry did so. And Mel asked another

question. "Were you on good terms with Dennis Roth?"

Imry hesitated just a second too long. "As actors go, he was okay."

"That's not what I asked."

"I'll be honest with you. I thought he was a good actor or I wouldn't have engaged him for this role. He looked the part. But I didn't much like his attitude."

"Why was that?"

"He didn't want to stick to the script."

Mel closed his notebook and said, "I'll be asking you more questions later."

When Mel confirmed that Imry's office had been gone over already, he went through the paperwork there and found the number for the registrar. He had to explain patiently that he was Detective VanDyne and that a student had been murdered. He needed the telephone number for his next of kin. He was told he had to come in in person and show his credentials.

"I'll send one of my officers. I need to be available here."

He called his office and told his assistant to arm himself with a badge and fetch the phone number for the victim's family and call him back.

When this was finally accomplished, he

rang the number. There was only an answering machine with a woman's voice saying, "We're out of town on our second honeymoon," followed by a silly giggle. "Leave a message and we'll get back to you." But the next voice was artificial. "This mailbox is full. Try again later."

The only thing Jane and Shelley learned from the early evening news was that the theater was indeed the site of the murder, and that a young actor from the local college had died under mysterious circumstances. The police were still trying to find the victim's family to notify them before a name would be released.

Mike and Katie had gone to fetch a Chinese meal for both families. Shelley's daughter Denise was still at her swim class. Her son was playing a new Nintendo game with Jane's son Todd at the Nowack house. Both Jane and Shelley were glad none of them were watching the news.

"So it's an actor. A young one. That excludes John and Gloria Bunting, and the director," Shelley said. "Still, it could be Joani. It's trendy to call both sexes 'actor' these days."

"You don't approve of that?"

"I do approve. I'm just saying it's not

necessarily a young *man*. But it could be that nice Bill Denk who plays the old butler, or Jake Stanton, who's the younger brother. Or maybe Denny Roth," Shelley said. "But it eliminates Professor Imry. He's not an actor."

"We know that," Jane said. "He's not much older than the students. The police might know his name but not necessarily that he wasn't one of the young actors."

"I suppose somebody could identify him, though. Whoever found him. Or her."

"It might have simply been someone from a janitorial service. Someone who wasn't ever around except when no one else was there, or just a botched robbery that went horribly wrong when the robber realized that somebody saw him."

Shelley shrugged. "I guess so. I wish Mel would call and fill you in a little bit. He knows, doesn't he, that we're tending to the catering?"

"I told him what we were doing. Or rather, that I was tagging along as a mere taster. But I only mentioned that it was a theater Paul had donated to the college. That's not all that specific. They must have some other buildings that previously served as at least rehearsal halls. Maybe we're wrong about where this body really is."

"That will be easy to find out. After dinner we'll drive by. If it's our theater, it will be surrounded by yellow tape saying CRIME SCENE — DO NOT CROSS; it will be obvious."

"You can do that if you want. But I don't want to be with you. Mel wouldn't like to see me snooping," Jane said.

"We could park a block or two away and just sneak a peek around a corner of some other building, couldn't we?"

"Shelley, get a grip. This is getting too elaborate. Mel will realize whether this is the theater where you're providing food. He's sure to ask us what we know about the cast and crew — when he's ready."

"Okay, okay. I give up. You're right. It's not any of our business unless Mel thinks it is. I'll have to tell Paul tonight, just in case the authorities need to know anything about the donation of the building."

"Where is Paul this time?"

"Doing a grand opening ceremony at a new restaurant in Dayton, Ohio."

"How many of his Greek fast-food restaurants are there now?"

"This is the forty-fifth. He always says it's the last one. He's starting to talk about retiring."

Jane laughed. "Don't let him do it,

Shelley. You and I both know several women with husbands who retired early. They hang around the house driving their wives crazy."

"I know. They all say the same thing. Every time the wife picks up the car keys, the husband asks, 'Where are you going?' Or tries to tell her a more efficient way to do the laundry, talking about how his mother always dried the sheets on a clothesline outside. They want to go along with you to the grocery store and the tailor. That would drive me wild."

She thought for a moment about this scenario and said, "I'm sure if Paul tried to retire, he'd find something else to do. Consulting with young entrepreneurs. Setting up a new business to try his hand at. Don't you think so?"

"I hope so for your sake," Jane said, patting Shelley's hand.

Chapter Eight

Mel called Jane just before eight o'clock the next morning. All she'd done since she'd heard the bad news was needlepointing. She couldn't bring herself to work on a murder mystery novel on a day when someone she probably knew, however slightly, had been killed. And the needlepointing didn't go as well as she hoped, either. She'd almost finished a big triangle when she realized the colors weren't right, and she would have to carefully pull all the threads out.

"Jane," Mel said, "this isn't for the public yet, but I'm calling on my home phone. Tell Shelley I've had a crew in overnight with flashlights, floodlights, little vacuum bags of hundreds of things that probably won't ever be relevant. Mostly candy wrappers and solidified chewing gum. We've gone over each inch of the main floor. They can resume the rehearsal tonight. We'll still be there, doing the basement, balconies, and the flies.'

"Shelley will be glad to hear this. She can alert the caterers in time. Mel, who was the victim?"

"Dennis Roth. Called Denny."

Jane sighed and said, "Thank goodness it wasn't Ms. Bunting or Tazz. I wasn't crazy about Denny, but it's sad when someone so young, with his whole life ahead of him, has it snatched away."

Mel said, "I understand that both you and Shelley have been sitting in on the rehearsals."

"Not the whole duration. We get there later than the rest of them, but before the caterers come. As soon as they've cleaned up and gone, so are we. Gone, I mean."

"Still, you've been there for — what? Half the time?"

"Pretty close to that. You can't imagine how boring it is. And how obnoxious most of them are."

"Denny in particular?"

"Not really. He was pushy and rude. But for sheer gall, the director, Professor Imry, is the worst."

"That's my impression, too. I've already interviewed him once. He turned up early yesterday afternoon."

"I was somewhat surprised, frankly, that he wasn't the victim," Jane admitted.

"He'd have made a good one." Jane could hear the smile in his voice.

"What have you learned about Denny?"

"All too little. He only enrolled in the college summer session after it was announced that the play was being put on and the Buntings were starring. Which means nothing. Lots of the cast and crew signed up around the same time. Nobody we've talked to so far knows anything about Denny's background. The college registrar says he claimed on his application that he'd only be there for the summer session. Gave credits for previous acting jobs that we can't confirm yet. The application said he currently lived in a suburb of Los Angeles. I've got someone there asking the neighbors about him."

"And — ?"

"Not much of anything. It's tacky furnished apartments, month-to-month rent, with all sorts of starving artists and actors who come and go nearly every week. Nobody so far admits to remembering him."

"So he really is a mystery man."

"What do you mean?" Mel asked.

"Just that you know so little about his background. Have you contacted his family?"

"I've been trying repeatedly, but all I get is an answering machine that won't take a message. As for knowing about his background, we'll know everything eventually.

It takes time, Jane." Mel paused. "I want your opinion on something."

That surprised Jane. "Ask away," she said.

"What's your view of Professor Imry? You've been around him longer than I have."

Jane thought for a moment. "Okay. A vast mountain of arrogance on the surface, and a small core of tasteless, suspicious gelatin underneath."

Mel laughed. "You should have been a writer."

"I am," she said indignantly.

"That was a joke, Janey. I wouldn't have put it that way, but you perfectly described my impression of him. He's like most bullies — soft and scared inside. My cell phone is ringing. Have to go. Thanks for your insight."

Jane was astonished. She'd given her opinions to and occasionally forced her suspicions on Mel before, but he'd seldom asked her to. Her remark was a good answer. She told herself to write it down before she forgot it, so she could use it again sometime in a book.

Having made a quick note to herself, she called Shelley to tell her that Mel said they could have the rehearsal that evening, even though the police were still looking for clues in the theater.

"Thank you for letting me know. I'll get back in touch with the caterers and tell them to show up tonight, as planned."

Jane went back to her novel. She was still working on the list of events, scenes, and motives that might or not work. She also wrote another chapter. The hours seemed to fly by. She suddenly realized that it was almost time to clean up and go to the theater. Where had the time gone? She'd wanted to fix that awful triangle she'd had to take out, thread by thread. Shelley was bound to be getting way ahead of her. Not that it mattered to Jane, but Shelley would rub it in.

When she arrived at the theater, everyone was sitting in the first few rows.

"Such a tragedy," Tazz said. "He was so young."

Jane wondered if Tazz was really older than Denny. She didn't look as if she were.

"I think we should say a prayer for him," Ms. Bunting said. "John, could you do that for us?"

John stood up facing the rest of them and said, "Lord above, please take your child Dennis Roth into your loving arms." For some reason it sounded stagey, as if it were a prayer he'd memorized from some play he'd been in.

"Amen," John added.

All but Professor Imry echoed the amen.

Then Imry cut in brutally, saying, "We're allowed to use these seats, the stage, the meeting room, and the kitchen. Nobody may go up into the flies. No one is allowed in the basement or balconies either. If you noticed, we still have quite a 'police presence' here."

He made it sound sarcastic. As if the police were silly to stick around.

"Now, let me introduce Denny's substitute. This is Norman Engel. He'll be playing the eldest son of Mr. and Mrs. Weston." He proceeded to start introducing the others by their script names.

"See here, young man," Ms. Bunting said. "That's offensive and unprofessional. We've told you this before. We're Mr. and Ms. Bunting except when we're on stage."

"Excuse me, Professor," Tazz said. "Isn't this Norman person the one that you said the day before yesterday was simply observing?"

"Yes."

"So you were going to fire Denny and replace him?"

A stunned silence followed this question.

Jane nudged Shelley and whispered, "That's what I thought but didn't want to say at that last rehearsal."

Imry pretended, badly, that he hadn't even heard the question. "Hadn't you better get on with your job? That's costuming. Not casting."

"I think I'm going to withdraw from providing the costumes," Tazz went on. "You can find them yourself." She picked up her belongings and started up the aisle.

"Wait. *Wait!*" Imry shouted.

"Wait for what?" Tazz replied. "An apology?"

"Yes."

Another long silence fell. Everybody was gazing critically at the director. "Get on with it and make it good, young man," John Bunting said.

"I'm sorry for what I said, Ms. Tinker." He said this so quietly nobody quite understood it.

"Speak up!" John barked.

"I'm sorry for what I said, Ms. Tinker!" he shouted. "Now let's all get to work. That's what we're here for, in case you've forgotten."

Tazz had returned to her seat, and now rose again. The rest of them also left their seats and followed her. All but Imry and his pet, Norman. Bill Denk muttered, "Exit to stage right."

"I'll sue every single person who leaves! You're all in violation of your contracts."

When the rest of them were halfway up the aisle to the lobby, a woman standing in the doorway stopped them. "Hold on," she said. "I'll get this sorted out. Go sit back down."

She spoke with such authority that they obeyed, albeit reluctantly.

The unknown woman followed them and approached the stage. "I'm Evelyn Chance. Remember me, Steven Imry?"

The cast and crew had filed back to their seats to hear what she had to say.

Ms. Chance went on, "I'm the person who helped the college solicit the funds to put this play on. I'm the one who's going to sue you for every penny I raised for this pitiful script, and for paying Mr. and Ms. Bunting, putting them up in the hotel, their airfare, their food, and rental car. I've also put in a lot of time promoting it, to my sorrow. Now, you will make a real apology, and mean it, to each and every one of us. Or we're all walking out and filing civil suits against you, you rude bastard. And keep in mind, too, that you are currently the most likely suspect for the murder of one of your actors. I've heard about him telling you off about your faulty grammar."

Imry all but collapsed, mumbling incoherently.

"Stand up straight, Steven. Don't be such a wimp," Evelyn Chance said.

Imry stood, shaking with fury. Jane spotted Mel standing on the edge of the stage behind Imry, making notes.

"I'm sorry. I'm really sorry. But you have no right to say I'm a suspect. I've never even thrown a rock at a bird in my whole life."

"Huh?" Shelley muttered to Jane.

He went on. "In spite of all of you misjudging me, I do apologize. I'm under a lot of stress here. This whole production rests on my shoulders. Don't you understand that?"

Ms. Chance stood her ground and said coldly, "That's not even a feeble apology. It's simply an arrogant attempt to justify your bad temper. I saw how you behaved the day before yesterday. Now start over and do it right."

Finally, after dithering, Imry started over and made a semi-real apology.

"I'm sincerely sorry if I offended anyone. As I said — no, never mind. I truly regret having been rude to anyone. The caterers, Ms. Nowack, and Ms. Jeffry. Ms. Tinker, Mr. and Ms. Bunting, Jake Stanton, Joani, Ms. Chance. Buddy Wilson, the head stagehand. Bill Denk, who plays the butler, and anyone I've left out by accident."

Then he turned and walked unsteadily up onto the stage and through the door to the workroom.

"I guess we'll have to stay," Tazz said. "Much as I regret it. I'd have liked to see him try to find the costumes by himself."

"And find caterers," Shelley added.

"And substitutes for us," John Bunting gloated.

Chapter Nine

When everyone had recovered from this scene, which was far more exciting and dramatic than anything in the script, the rehearsal went on. This time it was to work out where people stood or sat, or entered or left, in each scene. A sofa was represented by three chairs in a row, taken from the workroom. Three more of them represented armchairs. The placement of the doors was marked on the floors with chalk. Imry was subdued and relatively well behaved. When Bill Denk made another snide remark to the audience, Imry didn't even chide him.

Evelyn Chance was still sitting in the front row, and Imry kept giving her anxious glances.

Jane and Shelley took their needlepoint materials back to the workroom, after washing their hands as they'd been instructed. They left the door to the serving room open and the back door slightly ajar so they could hear when the catering truck arrived.

When they were seated in two of the remaining chairs in the workroom and had their canvases out, Shelley asked, "Do you think everyone who was threatening to walk out would have done so if Ms. Chance hadn't stopped us?"

"Wasn't she fabulous?" Jane replied. "I aspire to be that outspoken one day. Yes, I think they would have. All but Imry's replacement for Denny. Most of them are volunteers. Only Tazz and the Buntings stood to lose money. And there are probably others. I don't think you'd trust lighting to volunteers unless they were professional electricians and theater was a hobby."

"You're forgetting me, Jane," Shelley said. "I'd have been out on the deposits to the caterers. But if he'd continued to be so obnoxious, it would have been well worth it."

"Do you think he really learned anything about how to behave?"

"Not at all. He was just cornered and scared spitless."

"I wonder if Ms. Chance was right that he's the primary suspect for Denny's death? I'd guess that's what Mel thinks. Of course, I could be wrong about that. He never really said so," Jane qualified.

"Everything we know, which isn't much, seems to point to him," Shelley said. "My impression of him is that he's one of those bullies who knows deep in his heart that he's not as smart or talented as those he's bullying, and furthermore, thinks they won't realize it."

"It was unfortunate for him that he had a replacement lined up for Denny," Jane said. "And stupid besides. Denny was unwise, and was being a show-off by humiliating Imry in front of everyone, but the honorable thing for Imry would have been to fire Denny before choosing a successor. And Imry should have realized that Denny was right that Imry really should brush up on his grammar or hire someone to vet the script.

"On the other hand," Jane went on, "Imry didn't seem to have the kind of courage it takes to actually kill someone."

"It doesn't always take courage, Jane. Probably the fear of continuing humiliation could be enough to push someone as insecure as Imry to do something violent in the heat of anger."

"You might be right."

"Was that the sound of a truck?" Shelley asked.

"It was. I'll put your needlepoint things away for you."

That night's caterers were the most

imaginative, Shelley later declared. Along with colorful, sturdy plastic plates, they also had provided fruits and vegetables, meats and pastas, and sauces that were fresh and unusual. Broiled kiwi fruits with a mysterious tasty glaze. Tender scallops with lime sauce. Hot fingerling potatoes crusted with salt and some spice nobody could quite identify. There was also a creamy cooled rice salad with quartered green grapes, sliced blood oranges, and Vidalia onion chunks served with the best sourdough bread Jane had ever tasted.

"This is a lot more than a mere snack," Tazz said, helping herself to generous portions of everything.

"You get what you pay for," Shelley whispered to Jane.

Even Steven Imry complimented the caterers.

"Now, *that* sounded genuine," Shelley said to Jane in an undertone.

When the meal was over, and Shelley had watched the cleanup and filled in her forms, they said good night to the others.

"Want to stop at Starbucks for a cup of good coffee and a dessert?" Shelley asked.

"Why not? All I need to do at home is replace the nasty triangle I needlepointed earlier."

It was warm outside, but not as searingly hot as it had been earlier. They sat at a table where no one could overhear them.

"Did you notice that Mel was on the stage, out of sight of Imry, when Evelyn Chance took him on?" Jane asked.

"Yes, I did. He was making notes."

"Do you really think that Imry is capable of killing anyone?" Jane asked.

"I think so. But we really don't know anything about him, Jane. Where and how he was brought up. What he's like with friends — if he *has* friends. Our sole experience with him is when he thinks he's in charge of something dear to him. His awful script. The accolades he's anticipating from the audience and his college."

"Nor do we know much of anything else, and we'll never have the chance, or desire, to know him better," Jane said. "Probably Mel won't either. But Mel is the one entitled to ask hard questions and look into Imry's whole life. It will take a while, anyway, for the pathology report on the cause of death."

"Shouldn't that be easy? Look for a wound or test for poison?" Shelley asked.

"What if they find both? How would they decide what the primary cause was?"

"Good point. Of course, having seen the

body, Mel must have some idea of what might have killed him."

"Even if he does know," Jane said, "it might not help him figure out who was responsible."

"He'll find out eventually," Shelley stated. "He always does."

"But a few times we've managed to provide a clue not available to him."

"And you know how angry that makes him, Jane. I think we should probably stay out of this. It's not as if we're deeply involved with these people. We hardly know most of them. And when the two weeks of rehearsals are over, we're probably not ever going to see any of them again."

"Except for Gloria Bunting and Tazz Tinker, I wouldn't care. I like both of them. And while I admire Evelyn Chance, I wouldn't want to be chums with her. You don't have to keep catering when the production of this awful play starts, do you?" Jane asked.

"No. It won't start until seven forty-five. That gives everyone involved plenty of time to provide their own dinner before they go on stage. Now they have to be there at six, which is why they need the snack supper."

"Has doing this helped you with your catering problems?" Jane asked when they'd thrown their cups and napkins in the trash and started walking toward Shelley's minivan.

"Unless someone does a whole lot better than tonight's catering, this catering company is the one I'll use for Paul's employee dinners. They were only slightly more than the cost of the first two, and much, much better at presentation, taste, imagination, and timely, efficient cleanup."

When the rehearsal was over, Mel stepped out onto the stage and said, "I'm sorry, but you're all going to be a bit late getting home. I need to question everyone. I'll post an officer in the room with the big table and will summon you one at a time. You may use your cell phones, if you have one, to call home and warn your family."

Clearly no one liked this, Mel included. This was just the first set of interviews he'd do himself, and it had been a long day already. He had an officer sitting behind the interviewees taking shorthand notes on what was said.

The first person Mel called for was Norman Engel, the young man who was now the substitute for Denny's role. Mel gave him the standard warning. Norman said he didn't need an attorney.

He launched into his explanation without any prodding. "I'm one of Professor Imry's students. He asked me to turn up last night at the rehearsal. I had no idea why he wanted me there. So I obediently showed up. That's it."

"He didn't explain that you were to replace Denny?"

"Not a word. I went back to the dorm, wondering what the point had been. It wasn't until Imry called me early today that I understood. That's when he admitted he was going to drop Denny and replace him with me."

"He didn't mention that Denny was already dead?"

"Not until the end of the conversation. I'd told him I didn't think it would do my career any good to be secretly hired to replace another actor. That's when he told me that Denny had died, so I *had* to fill his shoes. Imry didn't even mention that it was murder."

"Had you known Denny Roth before this production?" Mel asked smoothly, not commenting on the murder.

"Not really. We were in one theater class together, but it was the one for all the students of the drama school. Not one of the small classes."

"What are your feelings about Professor Imry?" Mel asked.

"Not good ones. I never liked him to begin with, and when I learned what he'd planned to do, replacing another actor with me, I didn't like it. It's not professional."

"Thank you, Mr. Engel. If I have other questions, I'll ask them later."

The Buntings, together, were next. He gave the same warning, which they both waived. Mel asked them the same question he'd asked Norman Engel at the end of his interview. "Did you know Denny Roth before you got here?"

Both said they hadn't.

"What is your opinion of Professor Imry?"

Gloria Bunting fielded this question. "We learned early in our professional lives never to give opinions of our co-workers."

Mel had a grudging admiration for her speaking so plainly.

"Where were you on Wednesday night?"

John Bunting took over. "I was out late with old prep school and college friends." He named the bar and grill where they always met when he was in town.

"And you, Ms. Bunting?"

"Sound asleep. It had been a long day and I knew John wouldn't stagger in for hours."

Mel dismissed them and doggedly worked his way through the rest of the cast and crew. Nobody admitted to knowing Denny before the rehearsals started. Nobody liked Professor Imry.

When Jane arrived home, she tried to write another page or two of her manuscript, but her mind kept wandering back to the real murder. Everything Shelley had said was true. They didn't have enough knowledge of any of these people to even guess who had committed the horrible act. Professor Imry was, in both their minds, the primary suspect. Which wasn't really fair.

They'd made up their minds, as had most of the cast, that he wasn't a nice person. But that proved nothing. Lots of offensive people went through life without killing anyone. Hurting their feelings, yes. Maybe harming their career, yes, very likely. Though people like him, Jane guessed, never gave a thought to how much they'd harmed anyone with words alone.

Shelley was also right to say that Mel would find out about everyone's background, and that she and Jane should stay out of it. Even petty crimes often showed up in legal records. And if not, acquaintances remembered them. Mel would have to dig deep into everyone's lives, even those who weren't actors. Denny might have done something awful to one of the other people involved in the production. Stagehands, the volunteer students who were making the set. Even Tazz or Evelyn Chance.

On the other hand, Shelley and Jane had often provided information to Mel that only they knew. He'd seldom asked for their opinions. This time, he had asked Jane what she thought of Imry and even agreed with her. That made things different.

Or did it? Jane and Shelley, like others, didn't like him. But Imry wasn't the victim. He was the primary suspect. Denny Roth was the victim. And they knew very little about him. He wasn't much nicer than Imry. Though he'd committed only one offense they knew of, which was telling off Imry about his bad grammar in front of others. Hardly a good motive for Imry to actually kill Denny. Unless this criticism hit Imry in his heart and ego so hard that it unbalanced him.

She hadn't written a word. She had to stop worrying over this. Shelley was right. They weren't likely to become good friends of any of the people involved. The cast and crew would disperse in a matter of weeks. And Jane and Shelley themselves would step out of their involvement as soon as the rehearsals were over in another week. But she'd like to keep in touch with Ms. Bunting and Tazz, if she could.

Jane closed down her computer, went upstairs. She'd been so absorbed in her book that she hadn't been aware of the battle going on between her son and her daughter. Mike had his bedroom door open, music blaring. Katie was standing in the doorway, shouting, "I'm trying to talk on the phone. Could you hold the noise down?"

Todd, at his own computer, was staying out of the fray.

"Mike, Katie's right," Jane said. "Turn it down and close your door, please."

The din of drums and screaming lyrics died down and finally stopped. Jane prepared for bed and went back to reading a Martha Grimes novel she had somehow missed finding till now. It was a very early one, in which Jury and Melrose had met only one time before. How could she have not read it yet?

Chapter Ten

Mel called at ten-fifteen Friday evening. "Is it too late to talk to you?" he asked.

"It's never too late when it's you. I was reading a mystery novel I hadn't known existed. What's up?"

"I have the preliminary report from Pathology."

"Does it tell how he died?"

"Sort of. He'd taken some whiskey. Quite a lot. And tranquilizers. There's no way to tell, at least yet, if the whiskey had the tranquilizers in it, or if he took them at different times."

"No whiskey bottle?"

"No sign of one. Not a bottle of pills either. He was unconscious. He'd apparently put his head down on the makeup table in his dressing room. Then someone took something heavy and vaguely oblong to the back of his head. Crushed the connection to the spine and disabled all of his nervous system. He must have died instantly. The blood-spatter pattern indicated that his head was on the table when he was struck. But he might have died of the whiskey and tranquilizers anyway."

"How horrible," Jane exclaimed.

"Slightly better than being on a respirator and a feeding tube for life," Mel said. "If he'd been hit a little bit lower, that's what could have happened."

Jane thought for a moment, debating which of many questions she should ask. "Would this have taken a huge amount of strength?" was her first.

"It depends. If the perpetrator was strong and accurate, it could have happened."

"What else could it be?"

"Something like a pendulum. Not so heavy, but delivered with a swing of a rope or chain. Almost anyone could do that."

"I assume all such items have been looked for in the Dumpster outside?"

"The whole thing has been searched, of course. No sign of rope, chain, or a bottle of anything, just empty plastic cups and plates and empty water bottles. They've all been taken in to be tested for contents and fingerprints. Nothing that looks like an oblong weight."

"Wait a minute, Mel. How is the word 'oblong' being used?"

"What do you mean?"

"I once ordered a long rectangular tablecloth from a catalog, and when the package arrived it was labeled as being 'oblong.' Before I even opened it," Jane said, "I called the place where I ordered it and said that it looked rectangular in the picture. I was told that 'oblong' meant rectangular."

"I thought 'oblong' was a thing that was longer than it is wide, and curved into circles at the end," Mel said.

"So did I," Jane said. "Another perfectly good word trampled. 'Rectangular' is apparently not politically correct. Or maybe the people at the catalog thought they were synonymous — and maybe they are."

Mel was silent for a moment, then asked, "Who would have thought a murder could cross over into grammar? I'll ask the pathologist exactly what 'oblong' means to him. There is a weight missing."

"What kind of weight?"

"Something to do with raising and lowering the background scenery that goes up or down depending on the scene. Of course, there hasn't been a play there for a long time, and it could have been missing for years. Or only days. The young men who are painting the background of the room this play takes place in were looking for the rope and counterweight and couldn't find it."

"Would the missing weight be the oblong object?"

"Maybe. But if it had been there for a long time, there probably would have been signs of dust or rust in the wound."

"Was it a sandbag, maybe? Didn't old theaters use those?"

"I haven't the slightest idea," Mel said.

"Neither do I," Jane admitted. "It was just a fleeting thought. Probably because I saw some black-and-white movie that was set in a theater and a sandbag was dropped on somebody to kill them. Or maybe it was some mystery novel I read."

"Not through the ceiling of a dressing room, Jane." He said this with a hint of a yawn. "I'll ask about the definition of 'oblong' in the morning."

"Wait a minute. There are two things you haven't mentioned. Who found Denny and when?"

"The janitor from the college. He apparently comes in late at night or very early in the morning to replace toilet paper and paper towels, sweep the floors, and clean makeup off the counters in the dressing rooms before anyone's using the place. Around six o'clock in the morning, he said."

"How long had Denny been dead?

110

Could the pathologist tell?"

"At least since midnight. Maybe earlier. Why do you ask?"

"Just because I didn't know, I suppose. Does everybody connected to this play have a good alibi?"

"We're still questioning everyone. So far, almost everyone involved in any manner claims they do. Except you and Shelley. I've crossed both of you off my list of suspects," he said with a laugh. "But I'm always more inclined to believe the ones who admit that they simply went home and fell asleep in front of the television. Good night, Janey. Wish you were here with me. It's a nice cool evening for a change."

"Me too," she said with what she meant to sound like a kissing noise but ended sounding more like slobbering.

Jane went back to her book and found herself thinking about the murder weapon. It could be her definition of "oblong," but also rounded. So it could be a bottle. But a glass bottle would be sure to shatter if it were swung with a hard enough blow to break bones, wouldn't it? And a plastic water container would have burst. Surely the police would have noticed broken glass right away or puddles on the dressing table. Same for a sandbag. It would surely have lost some of the sand and the floor would have been gritty. She'd glanced into some of the dressing rooms early on and none were carpeted.

Not my problem, she kept telling herself, and went back to wondering about what the sharp double-pronged object that had killed someone in the book she was reading might have been.

She herself had a set of double-pronged sharp forks to lift a big turkey out of her deep roasting pan. But the book she was reading was set in Yorkshire, England, and there had been no mention of anyone cooking a huge turkey or an enormous roast beef.

She finally gave up on both the real murder weapon and the one in the book and turned the light off. An hour or so later, she rose again and turned on the attic fan while she was roaming around. The heat wave had finally broken.

Saturday morning, Jane stayed in bed late to finish the book she'd been reading, and found out what the weapon had been in the book. The clue had been well buried. She hoped she could bury her own clues that well. She went back to typing up a few other ideas for the book she herself was writing. None involved the weapon in the mystery she'd read.

When she'd put her new ideas into the outline and finished another half chapter, she cleaned up the mess the kids had made of the kitchen table, then succumbed to the lure of her needlepoint project. It took her a full hour to replace the triangle that had been such a failure before. And the canvas had lost some of its stiffness, so she had to be very careful not to let it stretch or sag.

There was another rehearsal already planned for Saturday. This time they wouldn't cater, because Shelley said most of the students didn't have late Saturday classes and could find their own dinners. She was only providing bottled water, a few sodas, a large carafe of coffee, and would bring along some chips or store-bought cookies.

But Imry threw another wrench into the mix. "Since we missed one rehearsal," he announced as they assembled, "I'm re-scheduling for Sunday afternoon from one to four."

"I'm sorry, but we're not available then. I'm spending Sunday with our daughter and grandchildren," Ms. Bunting said quite firmly. "I've promised to take them to lunch and the zoo since it's cooled down a little."

"And I'm committed to taking a group of schoolchildren on a walking trip along the lakeshore," Jake said. "They're inner-city kids I volunteer to take somewhere every Sunday afternoon."

Denny's replacement, Norman Engel, had other plans as well. He had his parents visiting from Indiana for a family wedding. Joani also claimed she was busy, declining to explain what the appointment was.

"Then we'll do it Sunday night. You can provide catering, can't you, Ms. Nowack?"

"Not on such short notice," she replied. "And the rest of the group will probably still be busy. Afternoon weddings go on forever. And anyone who takes on a mob of kids for a whole afternoon is entitled to rest later. I myself have other commitments as well. A bake sale at our church."

Jane looked surprised, then realized this was simply Shelley's way of thwarting Imry.

"Then we'll just have to meet earlier Monday, and work later," Imry said.

This raised another storm of protest. Most of the college volunteers were en-rolled in the intensive summer-school ses-sion, in which classes started early and went on until at least five-thirty to qualify for the credits for a full semester.

Imry was forced to give up — slightly. "Then we'll just add an extra half hour to each evening's work."

Apparently the people who had objected to Sunday had no good reason to object as strenuously to a half hour here or there for a few days.

"A bake sale?" Jane said as she and Shelley left the theater later.

"I thought it was an honorable excuse."

"I don't imagine anyone believed it," Jane said, eating the last two chocolate chip cookies that were left. "Didn't you see Tazz and Ms. Bunting exchange smiles?"

"I'm sure you're mistaken," Shelley huffed. "Probably neither of them has ever been to a church bake sale."

"But we've done our share of them," Jane said, tossing the paper plate into the trash.

Chapter Eleven

Mel came over Sunday morning to have a big breakfast with Jane and her kids. She'd really gone all out. It was what she called "a dining room meal." Not something to crowd around the kitchen table to eat.

There were homemade corn muffins, an egg casserole with scallions in a cheese sauce, sliced ham with a thick black-cherry sauce, and crispy baked new potatoes with rosemary, as well as orange juice for the kids and mimosas for the two adults.

Everyone was impressed and all the food was quickly gone. "That was wonderful, Mom. A long way from dorm breakfasts. You must have been down early to get all this done," Mike said.

"Nope. Most of it was made yesterday and just put in the oven at the right times to come out at the same time, fresh and hot."

Mike had to leave right after they ate. He was working again this summer at the garden center, and Sunday was their biggest sale day of the week. Katie was going to the town pool. She'd passed her life-saving course and was actually being paid to sit around and get a good tan. Jane didn't really approve of tans anymore.

"You must *slather* yourself with sunscreen," Jane said. "I'll drop in later and see if you're good and greasy."

"Oh, Mom," Katie objected, patting her mother's hand in a patronizing way.

Todd had arranged for two of his friends to come over and play games on the living room television.

"I should load the dishwasher," Jane said, "but it's such a nice day, let's finish off the mimosas on the patio."

"Are you going to use sunscreen?" Mel joked.

"No. We'll be shaded by an umbrella."

"I see that you've actually done some real gardening this summer. What kind of tree is that spindly one in the middle of the yard?" Mel asked, propping his feet on an extra chair.

"It's a bing cherry."

"I don't see any cherries on it."

"Mel, it's a baby tree. It probably won't get cherries for a couple of years. My grandmother had two of them when I was a kid. I'd visit her most summers. One time they produced so many cherries that she had to beg neighbors to come take most of them off her hands. The one requirement was that the cherries had to be bagged and weighed before the neighbors left. She actually gave away seventy-eight pounds of them. And kept ten pounds for her own pies."

"Eighty-eight pounds of cherries? I've never heard of such a thing."

"Neither had she. When she realized how many flowers the trees had, she hired two neighbor boys to net them so the birds wouldn't eat the fruit. I've never had a better pie in my life than she made."

She went on, "It did get two flowers this spring, but no cherries. So, how is your investigation of Denny's death coming along?"

"So-so. Not much information has come back on Denny himself. And I still can't manage to leave a message on his parents' phone. I've asked a cop in their town to go see if they're home. They're not. And none of the neighbors know when they're coming home.

"Tazz has an excellent alibi," he went on. "She was providing costumes for a private party. It was a reunion of a bunch of former hippies. Those who could still fit in their old clothes and had kept some, wore their own," he said. "Tazz dressed the rest of them who had wisely thrown all the tie-dyed stuff away."

"Was she there all evening?"

"Only after the rehearsal. She and her assistant dropped off the clothes some of them needed earlier in the afternoon, and went back after she was through at the theater to pick them up, examine them for food stains or sweat stains, and take them back to the warehouse well after midnight. Does she really make people who rent her clothes wear those underarm things?"

"She does."

"What if it's a sleeveless dress?"

Jane said, "I didn't think to ask. What about the others? John Bunting, for example? Was he alibied by his wife?"

"No. He'd been out to a late dinner after the rehearsal with a bunch of his old Chicago pals. They were finally asked to leave at midnight when the place closed."

"Did you interview all of them?"

"Yes, all but one of them, who is out of town. Are they ever a bunch of old coots. One has to carry his oxygen with him. Another is in a wheelchair and has a young man who accompanies him with his medicines. They're all successful old men. They either started companies here in Chicago or inherited companies from their fathers."

He went on, "One is called Bootsie. His father made expensive leather shoes and kept the shoe forms in storage, carefully itemized, until the client died. He claimed he always offered them to the bereaved family as a gift after the funeral. He's still in business. And he's the healthiest of all of them. Now he has fifty employees and they still keep the shoe forms. I'll bet each shoe brings in a fabulous profit. Handmade, hand-sewn, fitting perfectly and guaranteed to last at least fifteen years. Lots of his clients bring the shoes in after the fifteen years and want the exact duplicate.

"Another, 'The Pill,' inherited a pharmacy his father started in 1890 in the heart of the Loop. He showed me pictures of the original shop, with all the big bottles filled with colored water. At least I assume it was colored. It was a black-and-white picture."

"And the rest?" Jane asked, smiling.

"One, of course, is a lawyer. He didn't seem to have a nickname. He's retired and turned it over to his son and grandsons, but goes in every day to check out what they're doing. If I were a son or grandson of his, I'd have run away and become a cowboy or a plumber. He's the one who is out of town.

"The last one, called 'Big Buck,' is, you won't be surprised to learn, a banker. He started out as a pawnbroker and went on to found one of the biggest banks in Chicago, with branches all over the United States and most of Europe. Even a few in Asia."

"They must all be billionaires," Jane said.

"You're right. I was sort of surprised that they even let Bunting hang out with them. He's not a roaring success. And even if he's been in many plays and movies, he probably isn't anywhere near their financial league. But they all went to the same private grade and prep school at the same time, and men like that keep in touch, I guess. They've known each other virtually all their lives."

"I'll bet Bunting's appeal is that he's an actor," Jane said. "They can run old black-and-white movies for their great-grandchildren and say, 'I knew him as boy and man, and still get together with him.' "

"While the great-grandchildren snicker," Mel said with a grin.

"Maybe he made good money and was investing it well," Jane commented. "That might explain his friendships with the rest of the old dears."

"I don't think so. I called my mother . . ."

Jane kept herself from shuddering at the memory of meeting his mother once.

"She's a big fan of old movies," he went on. "She'd actually heard of them and looked them up in some of her reference books. She thinks he got his roles simply because he was the husband of Gloria Bunting. He usually played the silent, stoic husband the heroine doesn't appreciate, and she played the wife who has, or almost has, affairs with other men but always comes back to him, repentant and loving him all the more."

"I can imagine that well," Jane confirmed. "In the few scenes I've watched them rehearse, she *is* the character. He's nothing compared to her. He might have been good-looking, though, when he was younger."

"Maybe so. At least he carries himself well. Very stiff, but with a hint of dignity. Though my personal guess is that he's a big drinker and probably was quite a womanizer in his heyday."

"He's still attracted to young women," Jane said. She went on to explain that he sat down at the first reading next to the girl who plays the slut Denny brings home.

And that Bunting was trying to see down her blouse.

"His wife made him sit elsewhere. She must know that he's an old lecher," Jane said.

"Hmm," Mel said. "Maybe there is a sexual connection of a weird sort."

"Between who? Or should that be between whom?"

"You're the grammar maven, not me, Jane. What I meant was that Denny played the son who was marrying the slutty girl and Bunting took it to heart."

"It's a play, not real life," Jane reminded him.

"Not if Denny was really having an affair with the girl and Bunting was enraged."

"If so, he probably spends most of his life being enraged. He's an old man and can't compete with good-looking young ones. He must realize that."

Mel nodded. "I know I'm clutching at straws at this point. I'm still waiting for more information about all of these people. When and where they might have met before, whether they worked together, if they're old enemies of Denny's for good reasons. Don't worry. I was just thinking out loud. I've never made an arrest on a wimpy guess at who *could* have done it. I need solid proof.

"And in case you're wondering," he went on, "the slutty girl isn't acting. Everyone who knows her says she's just being her real self. Surly, sexy, and hopes to be the next Britney Spears. No talent. Just sexy. Also, the tough old cop who interviewed her found out that she was a great admirer of Gloria Bunting and said that she thought Ms. Bunting should have dumped her husband when she was young. Joani is a love-them-and-leave-them type. She wouldn't have murdered Denny for dumping her if they were having an affair. She's always the one to do the dumping. What's more, she told the cop who interviewed her, she'd never date an actor. All of them turn out to be obnoxious and selfish."

"Have you talked to the Buntings' daughter?"

"I have. She said quite frankly that if her mother had divorced him as soon as she, the daughter, was born, her mother could have been a real star in her own right. He held her back from some great offers of roles because there wasn't a role for him in them. Gloria Bunting could, the daughter says, have rivaled Helen Hayes in her prime. Even now, it's her mother that the grandchildren love. They have no interest in their grandfather at all. Nor does he show them any affection."

"How sad that is."

"Not necessarily. The kids love their grandmother, and so does her daughter. And to my mind, they're all happy enough with that. John Bunting doesn't enter into the relationships, and nobody cares anymore."

"What about the guy who replaced Denny?"

"I don't think he needs an alibi. He was invited by Imry to watch the rehearsal. He didn't know why. Imry offered him Denny's role, which he turned down because it would hurt his, Norman's, reputation to help Imry fill someone else's role. It wasn't until Denny died and Imry contacted him again, saying that Denny had died, that Norman agreed. And even then, Imry hadn't mentioned that Denny had been murdered."

"Another proof of what a jerk Imry is," Jane said.

As she spoke, her cat, Meow, hopped over the fence with a mole in his mouth. Jane leaped up, grabbed a shovel, and forced Meow to drop it, then threw it back over the fence into the vacant lot behind her own house.

Chapter Twelve

Mel and Jane had both become used to Max and Meow's feline hunting antics. When Jane sat back down, Mel said, "Joani Lang hasn't an alibi, exactly. She claimed she'd gone to a bar to meet a girlfriend who didn't show up. The bartender says she spent the time trying to pick up men. Apparently none of them suited her, or maybe vice versa. The bartender doesn't remember when she left. Or if she left alone or with some guy."

"Who else have you questioned?"

"Jake Stanton. He and his wife had a late dinner with another couple. They went home at ten-thirty and watched a movie. They described it and it was one I've seen. But it's not proof of an alibi — they could have watched it the day before. But I tend to believe them.

"Bill Denk says he just went home and read until he fell asleep. The prop guy, named Tommy Rankin, who has an antiques shop but likes theater, says he doesn't remember where he was, but says he wasn't at the theater that evening for sure. He'd been there earlier to get a fix on what he needed in the way of furniture, flowers on tables, and such. Same with the students who are painting the set. They both went home to study for their classes the next day. And that Chance woman was at a fund-raiser for another project. She and her husband went home around ten."

"Who else had keys?" Jane asked.

"There's a stagehand. Buddy Wilson. He says he wasn't needed until the dress rehearsal and never had reason to use the key and thinks he's lost it anyway. The lighting specialist and his two assistants, who are theater students, won't be needed until Monday evening's rehearsal. They did a preliminary study of the script and stage two weeks ago and checked that the equipment was working.

"You do understand," Mel went on, "that I wouldn't be talking to you about this except that you and Shelley have spent more time with these people than I have. I'm just letting you know my impressions so you two can confirm or deny them based on what you've seen and heard."

This was true. Mel had seldom asked Jane and Shelley for advice in earlier crimes when they'd been acquainted with some of the possible perps. That, of course, didn't stop them from sharing what they knew. He usually listened and didn't comment. Jane was flattered to be asked.

"We really only know about Ms. Bunting," she replied. "We've taken her to the needlepoint shop, and a lunch, and back to her hotel. We bought her a gift. Then the next day we took her to the needlepoint lesson. A nosy person asked her some personal questions, which she answered, and then she abruptly changed the subject back to needlepoint."

"What did she say about herself?"

Jane replied, "She'd gone shopping for her grandchildren and spilled baby toys out of her bag. The snoop asked if her daughter didn't have to be pretty old to have babies. Which was insulting. It seemed to me to suggest that Ms. Bunting is even older than she is."

"How old is she?"

"I really don't know. I'd guess early seventies. Ms. Bunting said she was in her early forties when she got pregnant. So the daughter would be around thirty."

"When I interviewed her daughter, that was what I would have guessed," Mel confirmed.

"Anyway, Ms. Bunting replied that it wasn't her daughter who was too old to have babies. It was she herself who had the daughter quite late in her life after three miscarriages when she was young."

Mel said, "That must have been a hard thing for her. Three in a row."

Jane was a bit surprised that any man could understand how difficult it might be to face miscarriage after miscarriage. She'd known several women who'd had one or even two and were devastated by it, fearing they were doomed to be childless forever.

"What did the rest of the people who knew Denny seem to think of him?" Mel asked.

"Shelley and I didn't like him. And when he bragged about being in a film at Sundance that won awards, one of the men said Denny had only been an extra."

"Which one said that?"

"I'm not sure. Shelley might remember. But it could just have been a guess anyway. Denny was very arrogant."

"What were your impressions of the rest of them? John Bunting, for example?"

"An old lech with bad breath," Jane replied instantly. "He made a point of sitting really close to Joani the first night," she went on. "She was wearing a really loose top and he was trying to get a good look at her breasts. Joani moved away from him just as Ms. Bunting told him to behave himself. He did know his lines, however. He sort of slurred them, but he had the words right."

"A heavy drinker?"

"Possibly. No. Probably. Did his old pals who got together say anything about his drinking?"

"They led me to believe they were all tanked by the time they left. I can't see how the rest of them are so successful in business if this is their usual alcohol consumption. But it might be Bunting's norm."

"I'd guess that's true."

Suddenly Mel changed the subject. "Since you fed me such a nice breakfast, let me return the favor. Let's go out to a really expensive restaurant tonight."

"You're on."

It wasn't to be.

Mel called her back at noon. "I'm going to have to back out of dinner. The janitor at the theater was found a while ago in the alley behind the same theater."

"Dead?"

"Not quite. In a coma. Not expected to survive."

"Same kind of weapon?"

"We don't know yet. The hospital is doing X-rays as we speak."

"I was looking forward to dinner, but I understand. I can occupy myself tonight with writing and needlepointing. Do get back to me when you know more, if you have time."

When she hung up, she called Shelley and told her about the janitor.

"Who would want to attack a janitor?" Shelley asked.

"I have no idea. Mel said he'd call me back when he knew more. Let's go get some good coffee and I'll tell you about the conversation I had with him this morning."

When they had their coffee and were sitting in a little park across from Starbucks, where no one could overhear them, Jane said, "For almost the first time, he asked what *we* thought of the rest of the cast."

"Amazing. What did you tell him?"

Jane recounted the conversation, including who had alibis and who didn't. Who had keys to the theater. Mel's impressions of the people he'd interviewed.

"Isn't that interesting. I know he loves you and tolerates me. It surprises me that he was so open about what he knew, let alone that he actually asked for our impressions of the people at the theater."

"I was astonished, too. We've nearly always had to force our opinions on him."

Jane took the last sip of her coffee and sighed. "I have to go home and do my two hours of writing and one hour of needlepointing. You know, I'm really enjoying learning how to work on a canvas more than I thought. It has nothing to do with words or plots. Maybe that's why I like it. It's a different sort of creativity."

"I know what you mean. It's much more interesting than rating caterers, figuring the taxes, buying groceries, and all the other boring things we're forced to do."

When Jane was home and at the computer, after checking the answering machine, which had no messages, she found herself wondering the same thing Shelley had. Why would anyone attack a janitor?

What do janitors do?

They clean up places when the people who occupy them aren't there.

That makes blackmail easy.

Mel was sure to know this, too.

She tried to put those thoughts out of her head and went back to her laptop to do her two-hour stint. She looked over her notes once more and made a note about butlers having the same access to private matters as janitors. Then deleted it. Two hours later she'd done another chapter. She was really on a roll today. She liked starting another chapter as soon as she finished one. It made her feel she'd gotten a head start on the next day. So she worked for another half hour. Then called Shelley again.

"No word from Mel. Want to needlepoint together for a while?"

"Okay. Here or at your house?"

"Mine. I want to be here in case Mel calls."

They sat down at either end of the long sofa in the living room, each having room for their thread containers. Both admired the other's work so far. Shelley's, however, was done a tiny bit tighter than Jane's. It figured, Jane assumed. Shelley was more intense in almost all matters than Jane was.

As they settled in to work, Jane explained her theory about janitors. "They work alone, and could get away with learning private things about people."

"I don't know," Shelley said. "There could be other motives, couldn't there?"

"Like what?"

"Maybe he was a gossip. Telling other people how sloppy his other customers were."

"That's not enough of a motive for attacking him," Jane claimed. "And how would the person who was slandered know about it? Or really care enough?"

"Okay. But what if he was stealing things?"

"Easy. You complain to his supervisor. You don't try to kill him to stop him."

"Maybe in self-defense, if the janitor was fired and tried to attack the person responsible for it."

"Maybe," Jane said, picking up the television remote and turning on Home and Garden TV. "I like my own theory best. But it doesn't matter. It's Mel's problem, not ours. Oh, this is my favorite show. *Designing for the Sexes*. I like that Michael guy. And you can always tell whose side he's taking. See? He's explaining, ever so nicely, why the man is wrong this time. But he'll be sure to provide one thing the husband really, really wants in order to pacify him."

Mel called around nine that evening. "The janitor has been in surgery almost all day, having pieces of bone picked out of his brain. There's a slim chance he may survive."

"Will he remember what happened?"

"Probably not. He may not really know anyway. The blow was to the back of his head. Most head injuries, I'm told, cause temporary or permanent amnesia. That's all I know now. I'm interviewing his supervisor in the morning about the janitor's normal schedule."

"You have thought about blackmail, haven't you?"

There was a long silence before Mel said curtly, "Of course I have."

"Sorry to ask. I presumed you had," she said cheerfully. "And don't forget, you owe me a really good dinner."

Chapter Thirteen

Early Monday, Mel had finally run down the woman in charge of the cleaning staff for the college. She was a surprisingly young Hispanic woman named Rose Havana. She had her dark hair in a neat bun and was dressed in a flattering blue suit.

"Ms. Havana, I presume that you know that one of your janitors, Sven Turner, has been seriously injured," Mel said.

"Yes, I know. I'm sorry about it. He's a good worker. Is he expected to live?"

"He might. The doctors aren't committing themselves yet. He's gone through a long operation and is still unconscious. His vital signs are improving slightly. That's all I know. Could you tell me about him?"

"Please take a seat. My coffee is ready. Would you like a cup?"

Mel nodded.

When she'd poured them both a steaming cup, she sat down behind her desk and said, "I don't know him well. I don't think many people do. I know he's good at his job. I frequently follow my staff members on their rounds to check that they're doing what they're supposed to. He is — or was — one of the most efficient."

"How long had he been employed by the college?"

She went to a file cabinet and brought back a folder. "He's been here for almost twenty years."

"Is there anything personal you could tell me about him? Family? Background?"

"Not really. He was probably the quietest person on my staff. That's why he liked being on the night shift. He didn't have to converse with much of anyone. He was very shy. If somebody on his rounds was working late, he'd call in to alert me that he was shifting the order of cleaning. Most of his work was here at the college. He only recently took on the job at the theater. I'm probably the only person he felt comfortable talking to."

"Did he call in at any time about the theater?"

"Yes, he did. A couple of days ago, he said he was at the theater. He'd let himself in and heard two men talking, so he was going back to the college and would do the theater cleanup early the next morning."

"Do you remember what night that was?"

"I'm sorry. I don't exactly recall. Maybe

last Tuesday or Wednesday. I don't keep records of things like that. Unless I know someone didn't show up to do their work, and the department that was neglected reports it."

She went on, "I guess the only other thing I know about him is that he always liked to get everything cleaned up early on Friday. He once told me he liked spending most of his weekends driving around in his car and visiting small towns."

Mel already knew that Sven Turner was forty-seven years old, and where he lived. The janitor hadn't been robbed and the information was all on his driver's license. Mel had already left a message for the local cop on that beat about going to Turner's home.

"Thank you, Ms. Havana. If you think of anything else we should know about Mr. Turner, please let me know." He handed her his card with his office telephone number.

She, in exchange, gave him hers and said, "Please let me know how he's doing, if you would. And would you get our van back to us? We're shorthanded with Sven gone and need it for what I hope will be a short-term replacement."

"As soon as it's been checked for fingerprints."

As Mel left her office, Police Officer Don Jones rang through on Mel's cell phone.

"Detective VanDyne, your office gave me your number. I've called on Sven Turner's sister and need your help. Or rather, she does."

"I'll be right there. I have the address."

It was in an old but fairly well-cared-for neighborhood near the college. When Mel arrived, Officer Jones was sitting on the front porch. Mel guessed Jones was probably in his late thirties and wondered why he was still on a routine neighborhood job. He was a tall, slightly overweight man, with a nice smile and very well-shined shoes. His uniform was perfection. Not a wrinkle to be seen.

Jones had risen hurriedly and opened the front gate. "Let me fill you in. I know Sven slightly. I know his sister better. She's homebound. She lost her lower legs several years ago to diabetes. I check on them from time to time."

"How's she taking the news?"

"Badly. She's dependent on him to cook for her. She's a single woman. We'll need Meals on Wheels and someone to clean and shop for her."

"Can she dress herself, get in the shower and bed by herself?"

"I'm not sure. You need to talk to her."

"Come in with me, then."

Hilda Turner was in her chair in the living room, which was spotless. Mel guessed this had probably been their parents' home. The wallpaper and carpet spoke of age. There were pictures of family members on side tables. She'd obviously been crying. Apparently Officer Jones had brought her a box of tissues and a wastebasket.

"I'm Detective VanDyne, Miss Turner. I'm sorry about your brother."

"Someone from the hospital told me a little bit about what happened to him. But not much. Could you tell me more?"

"He has broken bones in his skull and they've injured his brain. I don't know how seriously. The bones have been removed. He's still not conscious. I have to be honest with you — he could recover but not be entirely 'there,' if you know what I mean."

She looked a little confused.

Mel was forced to be blunt. "He might have permanent brain damage."

She started crying again, then made a bitter laughing noise. "What a pair we'll make."

"I'm going to get social services to visit you," Mel said. "They'll take care of you until we know more about your brother's condition."

She pulled herself together and said with dignity, "I'm not going on welfare."

"You will need help for at least a while. And it's not charity. It's what you pay taxes for. While I'm here, could I take a look at your brother's room? I don't know very much about him and it might help me find out who did this to him."

"Nobody but me knew him. He was terribly shy. Yes, you may look in his room if it would be useful." She pointed the way.

Jane spent Monday morning working on her book. She was enjoying writing this one much more than the first one, because she'd planned ahead instead of sitting down at random intervals and winging it over a long period of years. That technique had caused her an enormous amount of tedious rewriting. There had been times she hadn't even looked or thought about the book for weeks. Then she had to reread it all over again just to remember what she'd already done.

Of course, that time, she didn't know she needed to turn it into a murder mystery until she'd attended a mystery conference nearby and had the good luck to meet an encouraging successful writer, and an editor who urged her to send in the final draft.

She realized to her surprise that she'd spent several hours on it so far today. She also knew she had nothing to feed the kids or herself that evening. Even if she and Mel ended up going out for the good dinner they'd planned, she'd still have to leave something for the kids to eat. Or hand out a wad of money for Mike or Katie to get take-out. She hated going to the closest grocery store over the noon hour. There was a breakfast and lunch place next to it and parking places were at a premium.

Parking turned out not to be quite as horrible as she'd expected, and she came home loaded down with bread, sliced ham, premade tuna salad, several boxes of frozen mac and cheese, salad, and a really good, gummy iced chocolate fudge cake. That would last them for at least a couple of days.

She was on a countdown to school's starting. Katie would be in her first year of college, albeit close to home at the junior college for the first year. She had chosen it because it had several culinary classes. She'd still be living at home, but she could practice making dinners. Mike would go back for his third year of college, out of town, and Todd would become a sophomore in high school.

She loved her kids. She'd done a good job of raising them herself after her husband was killed on an icy overpass while leaving her to marry someone else. She seldom even thought about him anymore. After the first horrible months of grief and fury, she realized he'd freed her to live her own life, however inadvertently.

His life insurance included a rider that had paid off the mortgage on the house she loved. And due to her having given his family's pharmacy her small inheritance from a spinster great-aunt early in their marriage, he'd written in his will that she would forever earn his one-third share of the pharmacy profits. His widowed mother and his younger brother Ted received the other shares.

She realized much later that he'd been smart and canny about financial matters. It was morals that took him away.

The pharmacy had thrived and now had branches all over Chicago and far into the suburbs. Her share had allowed her to be a stay-at-home mom. This could have changed if he'd lived to marry the other woman. With years of parsimony and good investment advice, she'd put away enough to be able to get all three kids through college and finally, a year or two ago, had become financially secure enough to pamper herself a bit.

She was, she had to admit, proud of herself. And now that she believed that she'd eventually be published, she was prouder still.

Struggling inside with the groceries, then disposing of a few things that were past their prime in order to make room in the freezer, fridge, and pantry, she managed to clear the decks and go back to her needlepoint as a nice break. She realized, as she was getting out her threads to do the next section of her sampler, that she hadn't really thought about her deceased husband for years, and wondered why he'd come to mind today. She probably wouldn't think of him again for a good long time.

With luck, perhaps never.

Chapter Fourteen

As Mel was looking around Sven's room, which he wasn't surprised to find extremely clean, Officer Jones was conversing with Sven's sister. Mel couldn't hear what they were saying, except that Hilda was doing most of the talking.

The bedroom, besides being tidy, was revealing in other ways, too. It must have been his room when he was a boy. The wallpaper still had faded cowboys and horses. Even the single bed looked vaguely bunkhouse. It was probably the house both Sven and Hilda grew up in. Long ago paid off.

Sven was a serious jigsaw puzzle fan. There was a card table set up near the window with a half-done thousand-piece picture of a cathedral. The entire bottom of his closet was triple stacked with puzzle boxes, leaving only enough room for his shirts and trousers to hang above. His shoes were on a rack on the back of the closet door. They all looked as clean as if they were brand new.

So much for Jane's theory of blackmail,

which he had briefly considered himself. This was a shy, retiring, compulsively neat man with a shoe and jigsaw puzzle obsession. And he didn't like working with people watching him. Mel simply couldn't imagine such a timid man repeatedly approaching strangers and firmly demanding that they pay him for what he knew they'd done that was worth keeping secret. From what little Mel knew of him, Sven would be hard-pressed to work out the details of how to repeatedly receive the cash from someone.

Out of idle curiosity, Mel pulled out a loafer, its sole facing out. The shoe didn't look as if it had ever been worn. Something fell out of it that astonished him. He put the shoe and the object back. Next, he went to the upright chest that presumably held sweaters, socks, and underwear. He found more of what he'd seen in the loafers.

He was aware that although he'd been given permission to look at the room by the janitor's next of kin, he'd need a warrant to do more searching. He closed the dresser drawers and the closet door and went back to the living room. "I see that your brother really likes hard jigsaw puzzles, Miss Turner."

"He always has. He's always trying to get me interested in them, but they're all too hard for me to enjoy."

Mel said, "You gave me permission to look in your brother's room. Would you jot down a note saying so and sign it? Just as a formality?" He went on chummily, "So much paperwork is required these days, even by the police department."

He handed her his notebook, opened to the back page, and gave her his pen. He dictated, "To whom it may concern, I, Hilda Turner, gave Detective Mel VanDyne permission to search my brother's room."

The doorbell rang and Officer Jones went to open it. It was a neighbor woman with a brisket that smelled fabulous.

"Hilda, I heard about Sven. You poor dear. Nice to see you, Officer Jones. Hilda, I'll slice this up for you and bring back a salad and bread. Do you need anything from the grocery store?"

"Nothing yet, thanks, Susan. These nice men are going to see that I get Meals on Wheels. Oh, this is Detective VanDyne. He's going to keep me posted on Sven's condition." She handed the notebook back to Mel.

Mel noticed that Officer Don Jones was

easing his way toward the front door, waggling his eyebrows in a peculiar manner and nodding subtly toward the door.

Mel knew what this meant. "Miss Turner, Officer Jones and I need to go start arranging help for you and checking again with the doctors. We'll both be back."

As they left, Mel heard the neighbor Susan say, "That detective is a good-looking man and a snappy dresser. I could go for him."

Once outside, Jones said, "Come sit in my car and we'll drive around the corner. I have things to tell you."

"So do I," Mel said.

"Miss Turner started telling me about their finances," Officer Jones said. "She had a good job for years, and when she became ill, she was given an excellent severance package. She's also getting money from her social security for disability. But get this — she says Sven is a professional gambler. Almost every weekend, he leaves her prepared meals and goes to Indian reservation casinos in Minnesota or the casino boats in Iowa or St. Louis."

He went on, "She says he's good at blackjack and bingo. And he always stays under the limit of winnings that have to be reported to the IRS."

Mel was nodding.

"You're not surprised?" Officer Jones asked.

"Let me tell you what I found in his room," Mel said. "He had a huge number of shoes in one of those hanging things on the back of his closet door. I picked out a loafer that looked as if it'd never been worn, and out fell a tidy roll of hundred-dollar bills. Same thing under his socks and T-shirts. That's why I had Miss Turner sign that statement that she'd given me permission to look over his bedroom."

"You couldn't have surprised me more if you'd kicked me in the head," Jones exclaimed. "They seem to live so frugally and modestly in that old house. It's the original wallpaper and carpeting, it looks like to me. Do you think *all* the shoes were full of cash?"

"I didn't think I should look further without a warrant. Miss Turner isn't going to like that."

"I think Miss Turner is telling us what Sven tells her," Officer Jones said. "And it's not the truth."

"I agree. If I hadn't heard from his boss and Miss Turner how shy and antisocial he is, I'd be thinking about blackmail."

"That was my first thought, too, when you told me about the shoe."

Jane had left a message on Mel's cell phone. "Give me a ring and tell me what you've learned about the janitor if you have a moment free."

He called her back as soon as he'd applied for the warrant and asked for a police officer rotation to guard the hospital room Sven was in for twenty-four hours a day. If it was blackmail, one of his victims might drop in to make sure Sven didn't survive.

"I know more about the janitor than I want to know or understand yet."

"What do you mean?"

"I'm not allowed to tell you. But his blood pressure is getting better, he's moving a bit and making sounds. He'll probably survive. Whether his thinking and memory are seriously impaired can't be known yet."

"Not allowed to tell me?" Jane asked, a bit put out. He'd suddenly lost the urge to be forthcoming.

"That's right. You might know eventually, but not yet. I have a lot on my plate today. I'll try to catch up with you later."

There was well over a hundred and fifteen thousand dollars hidden in Sven's room. In every shoe there was cash. Rolled bills were hidden in sock balls and even stashed in puzzle boxes.

Miss Turner was furious when Mel told her it would have to be at least temporarily confiscated for her own safety. "It was counted out by several law officers. Sometimes this large an amount of cash is tempting. Not that I believe any of the officers are crooks. But not all of them are close acquaintances of mine. You might find yourself being robbed."

"But where's the money going?"

"Into a safety-deposit box. I'll call for an armored car to take it. Now, you must count the bundles yourself to assure that it all comes back, if circumstances prove that it really belongs to you and your brother."

"Of course it does. I'm just surprised at how it's added up."

"I'll open each bundle and you flip through, counting the hundreds," Mel offered.

"That would take me days. I'm going to have to trust your people to at least know how to count money."

"I wish you wouldn't. But I can promise you this — I watched every single bill counted and bundled, and nobody took a single bill."

"Then you can call your truck and give me a receipt."

"Gladly," Mel said.

Jane had called Shelley after her conversation with Mel. "Our source of information has dried up. Mel called and said some weird things about knowing about something he didn't quite understand yet and couldn't talk about."

"That sounds fascinating," Shelley said. "Why do you suppose he said he didn't quite understand it yet?"

Jane shrugged. "I have no idea. He did add that someday he might be able to tell us about it."

"I hope so. I hate teasers that are never revealed."

"So do I. I'm so glad this whole play thing will soon be out of our lives. Who are your caterers this time?"

"The ones I had to cancel earlier. They agreed that with sufficient time to prepare, I wouldn't lose my deposit. Which is sensible. We only have to go to the theater for four more days, including tonight. I was wrong about the opening night. The play doesn't start until seven on Friday, so the cast and crew have time to find their own dinners."

Rehearsals resumed on Monday evening. Since the second crime had taken place outside the theater and involved someone none of them admitted they'd ever met, the practices didn't have to stop. Everyone had been questioned about whether they'd ever been in the building when the janitor was. Nobody, it appeared, was aware that there *was* a janitor.

Shelley was trying out yet another catering company, and was extremely unhappy with them. They were late to arrive. The food was bland and skimpy. They barely cleaned up after themselves. Jane suspected that the owner would receive a piece of Shelley's mind before the evening was over.

The background scenery was finished and done well. It truly looked like an elegant room. It had a sense of depth. The man who supplied the props had been in earlier and set up chairs, a sofa, rugs, lamps, and tables with ornaments, books, and flowers. The fireplace, which had a narrow mantel, was strewn artfully with what looked like genuine old family pictures in black-and-white and even sepia.

Seeing things coming together well had

apparently made Professor Imry slightly less offensive. His goal was in sight at last, Jane assumed. She settled in a chair in the front row of the theater to work on her needlepoint, but she soon realized there wasn't a good enough light to make color choices. So she put her supplies away and took her "emergency" paperback out of her purse.

Jane didn't go anywhere without a book to read. Not even on short drives. She'd once been caught in a traffic snarl that clogged a whole lane because a truck was on its side. All she'd had to read in the car was a Horchow catalog, which she had practically memorized by the time she could creep far enough to take a side street.

There was enough light to read an old Ngaio Marsh paperback while Shelley was probably on the pay phone in the lobby, tearing a strip off the owner of the catering company.

She was also half watching the rehearsal. It was interesting to her that the book she was reading also took place in a theater. This rehearsal seemed to be going well. Everybody knew their lines. Nobody but the butler, who was still making side remarks, flubbed a single one. Ms. Bunting was wonderful. This pleasant woman in real life playing a nasty old woman was amazing to watch. Denny's replacement was barely okay. He, like Imry, didn't have an appealing personality.

But nobody else really sparkled. How could they with such a dreary, stupid, humorless, pointlessly plotted script? For a moment, Jane felt a tiny bit sorry for the director/scriptwriter Imry. She wondered if there would even be a second performance.

Mel was starting to have doubts. Both Sven's boss and his sister, who knew him best, had claimed he was too shy to talk to strangers. There was no good reason to doubt either woman's judgment. Maybe the blackmail theory was, in fact, wrong. Could a timid person like Sven muster the courage to blackmail anyone? He didn't seem to have the nerve to even speak to strangers. He couldn't imagine Sven confronting anyone repeatedly for cash, much less arranging for where and when the cash would be exchanged.

On the other hand, Mel knew he'd clearly done the right thing by seizing the money for the time being. He'd put an extra officer on duty watching the Turners' house, just in case word leaked out that it was full of cash. Everybody involved in counting the money knew that it had been removed. That might not discourage a neighbor or one of the people who did the counting from thinking they might have missed some of it.

Could a man in his forties and his sister in her fifties have genuinely stashed away that much money? It was possible. Apparently Hilda had once had a well-paying job. She could have turned her earnings over to her brother. And the story of Sven's gambling could be accurate. Hilda had also told Officer Jones that neither she nor her brother had children or had ever married.

The Turner siblings certainly hadn't spent much on themselves or the house. It seemed stuck in the late nineteen-fifties. Same wallpaper. Same paint. Same old-fashioned kitchen and bath, though the bath had handicapped equipment installed. That wasn't a frivolous expense, it was a necessary one. They could simply be the most frugal people in the world. Who or what were they saving the money *for?*

Chapter Fifteen

Having taken care of Sven and Hilda's situation for the time being, Mel turned his attention back to Dennis Roth's murder. He made his fifth try at the Roths' answering machine, which again didn't work. Two different cops in the suburb the Roths lived in had tried to find a neighbor who knew when they might be home. Apparently the Roths weren't sociable enough to have told them. As he cruised through the paperwork one last time, he found that one of his researchers had discovered that Denny was adopted. But the original birth certificate wasn't available.

It wasn't much help. It might be possible to do a search of some sort for a baby named Dennis born on the same date, which might lead to a birth certificate. But what would that prove? Just that he was probably born illegitimate.

The background check of Professor Imry was just as useless. Born three years earlier than Denny in a small town in western Oklahoma, he'd gone to grade and high school there, then went to Chicago to the university that now owned the theater. His grades all through his life had been high C's and low B's. Medical records showed nothing out of the ordinary except one episode of asthma. Census records in Oklahoma merely gave information that his father was a Nazarene minister and that his mother was a housewife a few years older than her husband. Both parents had been born in the same town as their only son. There had been a sister named Carol two years older than the boy.

The Buntings were harder to trace. All that could be found was their theater and film credits. He wondered briefly if their name was really Bunting, or if they'd chosen it because it sounded and looked good on the credits. No arrests, no birth certificate in any state for John Bunting. And no record of his wife's maiden name. He debated over asking them outright what their real names and dates and places of birth were, but he decided it probably wasn't worth the trouble. Ms. Bunting obviously was too small and frail to have delivered the lethal blow. And John Bunting, who was usually drinking, wouldn't have had the coordination to do it accurately.

Joani had one record for soliciting three years earlier. He wasn't surprised but didn't think she had the strength or motive for killing anyone, let alone an actor she had probably never met until the first rehearsal.

The rest of the cast and crew were exactly who they said they were. No criminal records. Only a few parking violations and speeding tickets.

Imry himself was still his prime suspect. Growing up in a small town in the back of beyond with a minister father must have been horrible for him. He obviously craved fame and fortune in the arts, even though his lack of talent and unpleasant personality seemed to doom him to failure.

Even Sven and Hilda Turner were more interesting than Imry was.

At this point, Mel was becoming slightly discouraged. Gathering fingerprints, background information, and scraps of possible evidence was slow and tedious, and ninety-nine percent of it wasn't relevant. It wasn't all that unusual for a case to proceed slowly unless the criminal was stupid or caught red-handed committing the crime.

Often there was simply too much information to absorb at once and make connections. Census reports, title searches, and examinations of property taxes were often farmed out to professionals in those fields. Then there were transcripts of all the interviews that had been conducted by other officers.

Like most experienced detectives, Mel had his own way of working through the masses of paperwork and figuring out problems. First, he read through all the reports again and again. Items found at the scene of the crime, information revealed in background checks, questions asked, and the answers given.

He made notes in the margins of anything he found remotely interesting. Most important and time-consuming, but most valuable, was the process of reinterviewing people other officers had interviewed and asking different questions. Quite often unexpected questions triggered more memories. Often people who had been interviewed later thought of something they saw or knew that seemed too trivial to bother reporting. Most of the interviews his subordinates had conducted didn't include a vital question: Had you ever met Dennis Roth before this play was cast?

Jane received a long-distance call that afternoon. It was from a 212 area code, and her heart skipped a beat.

"This is Melody Johnson. Have I

reached Jane Jeffry?"

"This is she."

"I have good news. Please pardon the slight delay. I've passed copies of your book to a few of the marketing people, just to show them why I'm so eager to buy it. They loved it as much as I do."

Jane was speechless for a moment.

"Are you there?"

"Yes. It's just such a wonderful surprise that it took my breath away for a second. Do you want changes?"

"That's your first question?" Melody said with a laugh. "No."

"So where do we go from here?" Jane asked. "You realize this is my first book sale."

"I'd like to work out the details of the contract with an agent. Do you have one yet?"

"No, I don't."

"I dislike dealing with a first-book author who doesn't know the ropes and might suspect she's not getting what she deserves. Would you like me to suggest some agents?"

"Could you wait a day for me to ask Felicity Roane about this? She's the one who encouraged me so strongly to submit it to you."

"That's a good idea. Then we can compare our lists. Congratulations, Jane. You're going to be published. I know how important this is, especially the first time. Get back to me as soon as you can find Felicity. Here's my telephone number."

Jane knew it was on her caller ID, but she was afraid she'd push the wrong button on the phone and lose it. She wrote it down on the back of her grocery list.

After dancing around the house, singing, "I've sold a book, lucky me," she transferred Melody's number to her address book so she wouldn't lose the shopping list.

Now the big question was who to tell first. Shelley? Shelley would be the most thrilled. But maybe she should tell Mel first. Or her kids. But none of them were home. Finally she decided the first call should be to Felicity Roane. Felicity had given Jane her card with her real name and home and cell phone numbers written on the back. Jane had that in her address book as well. Felicity might be hard to run down.

Fortunately, Felicity was at home. Jane introduced herself and Felicity said, "You've sold your book, I'll bet."

"I have. Melody Johnson wants to buy it.

She also wants to deal with the contract through an agent."

"Of course she would. It's best for her, and also for you, to do it that way."

"She told me she had three suggestions. I told her I wanted your suggestions as well before we decided."

"Did she agree?" Felicity asked.

"She did."

"Okay, do you have paper and a pen handy?"

"Yes, go ahead."

Felicity listed three good mystery agents who were heads of their own agencies. One was her own. Then she went on to list five agents Jane should *not*, under any circumstances, contact.

Jane thanked her effusively and said she'd let her know which one she picked to be her agent — if any of them wanted her.

She called Melody Johnson back. "I've talked to Felicity already. These are the names she gave me." She read them out.

Melody laughed. "Exactly my list. I'll try Felicity's agent first since Felicity is so happy with her. Thanks for being so prompt. If you want to look the agent up, her name is Annie Silverstone, and you can go to her website." She spelled out the letters slowly so Jane could write it down exactly.

The next call was to Shelley. "Guess what?"

"You sold your book! I could tell from the way you screamed the words."

"I have," Jane said in a slightly calmer voice, then told Shelley about Melody Johnson wanting Jane to work with an agent on the contract terms. She added that she'd called Felicity and that Felicity had suggested the same names Melody did.

"I'm hanging up to come over and hug you to death," Shelley said. And she very nearly did.

"I still have to tell Mel."

"And your kids."

"None of them are home right now. Shelley, I know this is sort of stupid, but I don't want anyone else besides Mel and the kids to know about this."

"Why?"

"I'll tell the earth when it's actually a book. Not a manuscript. I'm afraid of jinxing it by blabbing too soon."

"Jane, how can you swear me to secrecy about something this important? I want to brag on my best friend. I'm so proud of you!"

"Then you can tell your family, but no one else, okay?"

"Everyone in my family and Paul's? That's quite a few people."

"Most of whom won't be the least interested," Jane said with a smile.

"What about the needlepoint group?" Shelley was like a dog with an especially tasty bone.

"Only Tazz and Ms. Bunting, please. And we'll tell them at the theater."

"All right. I'll go home so you can tell Mel privately," Shelley said.

Mel, still deep in paperwork, answered his office phone briskly. "What's up, Janey? I'm really busy."

"Not too busy for good news?"

"I guess not," he said, still rustling through papers.

"I've sold my book. Well, sort of sold it. I need an agent to negotiate the contract."

She heard the thud of a big pile of paper. "Way to go! That's wonderful. I've always known you'd do it."

"If you knew that, I sure didn't."

"I'm working right now. But I'm leaving early. Dig up your fanciest clothes and we'll have that fabulous, expensive dinner tonight."

"I can't do it early. I need to tell the kids

when they all come home. And then I have to be at the theater, tasting things."

"The later the better," Mel said. "More romantic. I'll pick you up at eight-thirty, if that's okay?"

Chapter Sixteen

The kids were genuinely thrilled that their mother had actually sold a real book to a real publisher. They all hugged her. Katie was even a little tearful. "I can't wait to tell all my friends."

"Oh, please don't tell them yet," Jane said. "I don't even know enough about what happens next. Wait until there's a real book with a cover to show them."

"When will that be?"

Jane admitted she had no idea. That wasn't even something she'd considered. And it hadn't been something she'd heard at the mystery conference or even knew to ask. Come to think of it, there were suddenly a lot of questions, and she wished she knew someone who could answer them.

"Are you going to make a lot of money?" Todd asked. Jane had known one of them would ask her this. She had expected it to be Katie.

"I have no idea yet. I don't know if it will be a couple thousand dollars or a lot. My guess is maybe five thousand. Maybe a little more."

167

"But you'll make more on the one you're writing now, won't you?" Mike asked.

"Well, I certainly should. That's the way it's supposed to work, I understand. But I think you need to write a lot of them, and get lucky on the sales, before you make a whole lot more. But I'll bring you up to speed when I know more."

"Who have you told?" Katie asked.

"My writing friend Felicity. Shelley. Mel. And you three. I might tell two other people privately. Ms. Bunting and a woman named Tazz."

"The secret expands," Mike said with a smile.

"Eat your sandwiches. What are you all doing tonight?"

For the first time this summer, none of them had much to do. Katie said, "I'm trying a new recipe I learned in summer school. It's a dessert. So Todd and Mike have to stay home to eat it. Why aren't you eating anything now?"

"I have to go to the theater again. Just to taste what food Shelley's caterer comes up with, then rush home and dress up to have a really fabulous meal with Mel. He's been promising me one and he's finally tearing himself away from his desk to supply it. I'll be out late — we're not leaving until eight-thirty. If you go somewhere, leave me a note about where you are and telephone numbers."

"I'll leave you a piece of my dessert with the note," Katie said.

Jane and Shelley drove their own vehicles to the theater. Jane had already explained why she needed to leave early.

"If I were you, I wouldn't even have turned up," Shelley had told her. "It's a good thing to have an excellent celebration dinner with Mel."

"I promised to help you taste things."

"You can leave after a teaspoon of each snack. Then bolt home and dress to the nines."

Jane, naturally, had arrived a little later than Shelley, even though Jane had pulled out of her driveway first. She often wondered why Shelley didn't get her driver's license revoked regularly. But Shelley had never been issued a speeding ticket while Jane was riding with her — her own foot constantly pressing on the imaginary brake on her side of the van.

This was almost the end of rehearsals. Wednesday night would be a rehearsal with all the real furniture and lighting. Thursday was the formal dress rehearsal, and

Friday was opening night. Shelley had insisted up front that the college arrange for drinks and any food they'd like to sell at the intermission. On Thursday there would be a mob to feed. In addition to the cast, there would be Tazz, the stagehands, the prop master, the lighting director and his two students, and Evelyn Chance with three of her biggest contributing investors.

The front of the building was covered with posters, the college was probably awash in posters, and the box office was open and selling tickets already. Fortunately the box office people didn't have to be fed. Evelyn Chance was probably the only person involved in the play who had worked on Sunday. She must have been busy slapping posters everywhere.

Jane went looking for Ms. Bunting during the one scene in the first act that she wasn't in. She found her in the workroom, needlepointing.

"Yes, before you ask, I washed my hands first," she said.

"I have a secret to tell you," Jane said. "Because I like you so much. I just sold a mystery novel this morning and I promise it's better than this script."

"Oh, Jane, that's wonderful news. Is it a real publisher?"

"It is. And a good editor. I'd like to know an address for you so I can send you an autographed copy when it comes out. I hope you'll like it."

"How sweet of you. I'll keep your secret. Are you telling anyone else here?"

"I thought I might tell Tazz. I like her, too."

"She'll probably be as thrilled as I am for you. Do you have something I can write my real address on?"

Jane fumbled around in her purse and finally just ripped a deposit form out of her checkbook. "If I ever get business cards, I'll have them made to look like check deposit forms," Jane said.

"With your sense of humor, I know I'll love your book," Ms. Bunting said, neatly writing her address on the back.

"Now I have to tell Tazz," Jane said.

She found Tazz sitting in an audience chair wearing a lighted magnifying mirror on her head and repairing a tear in the hem of one of the costumes. She put the dress aside and took off her headgear. "You look like the cat that ate the canary. So happy."

"I am. I have a neat secret that I'm only telling you and Ms. Bunting. I've just sold an historical mystery today. I worked on it for years and I have a head start already on the next one. I'm really feeling smug."

"And so you should. And maybe you can help me. I've always meant to write a book about being a costumer. I think a lot of people would like to read it. I've made notes. How about you write it up for me and we share the profits evenly?"

Jane felt as if she'd been slapped upside of her head. She thought for a moment and said, "I wouldn't have the time to do that. Making notes is just a starting point. Writing it is what counts. You need to write it yourself if you care enough."

"Oh!" Tazz said. "So sorry you feel that I imposed on you." She snatched up the dress and put her lighted magnifier back on her head. As Jane got up to leave, Tazz added, with clear sarcasm, "Congratulations."

You won't be getting a free copy, Jane thought, close to tears.

When she returned to the workroom, the snacks were being set up. Ms. Bunting was putting her needlepoint paraphernalia away. "Oh, my dear. You look as if you've been kicked in the head. And you were so chirpy earlier. What's wrong?"

Jane told her about her brief, annoying conversation with Tazz.

"I almost warned you not to tell her. Now I wish I had. She's a strong-minded, bossy young woman. She told me — quite gratuitously — that I needed to gain some weight or pad my bosom."

"No, you don't," Jane said, shocked at this example of rudeness.

"I told her it was none of her business," Ms. Bunting said.

"I more or less told her I couldn't be bothered to write her book for her."

"Good for you! Forget her. There will be others who want the same thing. A free ride and a full share of the profits. I can't tell you how many aspiring actors of both sexes have demanded that I make sure they get the part they want. I tell them I'm an actress, not an agent. Go find an agent and pay them for their help if you're any good at this. They never ask me again."

Shelley came out of the small kitchen and announced that snacks were ready, and when she saw Jane, she asked, "What's wrong?"

Jane quickly summarized her conversation with Tazz.

"No! What a hell of a nerve, if you'll forgive my language, Ms. Bunting."

"I said almost the same thing. In the arts, especially, everyone thinks you're a public charity and owe it to them to help you. Mediocre singers want good singers to teach them for the sheer joy of it. I know graphic artists whose local grade schools expect them to decorate their blackboards just because they should contribute to the public welfare. And some of them actually do it. Poor dolts."

Tazz didn't speak to or look at anyone while she picked up her snacks and took them back to her seat in the theater to eat alone. Jane took a teaspoon of everything and pronounced it slightly better than okay. Shelley nodded her agreement. "Out of all I've tried, only one was superior. I'll probably hire them for Paul's next employee dinner. Now, Jane, run on home and dress up. Forget Tazz. She's not the nice person we thought she was. We were simply misled."

Mel picked up Jane, saying how glamorous she looked in emerald green as he opened the door of his red MG for her. "You sounded so excited this afternoon. Why aren't you now?" he asked as they started out.

"I'll tell you when we get to the restaurant. Somebody hurt my feelings. I'm almost over it. I'll talk about it once more, then cast it out of my mind."

When they reached the most elegant restaurant in town, the owner himself showed them to a lovely private booth. Mel ordered wine, the maître d' showed up next to welcome them, and a waiter snapped open huge napkins and flipped them on their laps.

Mel leaned forward, gestured for her to hold his hand, and said, "Tell me."

Jane recounted her conversation with Tazz. Mel frowned and said, "Forget she exists. I was frankly surprised that you claimed to like her. I didn't."

"You have better judgment than I do, I guess," she said curtly, then put her other hand over her mouth for a moment before apologizing. "I'm sorry. That was snarky."

"Oh, I don't blame you for feeling snarky, Janey. But I *do* have better judgment about nasty people, because in my job I meet so many of them. It sounds to me like you won the battle, not her. I'm glad you put her in her place."

Jane smiled. "You're right. She's not worth fretting about. She was trying to take outrageous advantage of me, and I did put her down firmly. I did win. Thank you for your opinion. Shelley and Ms. Bunting said sort of the same thing, but it means more coming from you."

Their wine arrived. The waiter had been watching closely for them to disengage their hands and finish whatever they were talking about that seemed so intense. The first second he could, he brought their wine and returned immediately with menus the size of Rhode Island. A moment later he delivered crusty rye rolls with a frigid plate of fancy curls of butter. Jane and Mel were invisible to each other as they studied the menus.

"Let's decide now so we can get rid of these monster menus," Mel said. "Let's go all out. Appetizers, salads, entrées, and desserts."

"I don't think I could eat that much. Could we drop either the appetizers or the salads? I'd prefer salad."

Mel signaled the waiter and placed their order, then took a roll and slathered it with butter. "I don't have to eat this immediately. I'm just buttering it while it's hot."

"Good idea," Jane said, doing the same. "Can you explain yet what you said you'd discovered and didn't know what it meant?"

"I still don't know what it means, but I can tell you the details. Maybe something will ring a bell and you'll solve the mystery of the janitor and his sister, the janitor's shoes, and jigsaw puzzles."

Jane laughed. "I'll give it a try."

Chapter Seventeen

"Start at the beginning," Jane said.

Mel thought for a moment. "The janitor, Sven Turner, called in to his supervisor the night he was supposed to clean the theater late at night. He said he'd heard two men talking, so he decided to go back early in the morning."

"What difference did it make if two people were there?"

"First, one of them was Denny, and it was the night he died. I have no idea who the other was. But most important to Sven was that he didn't like being around people. That's why he took the night shift almost all of the time."

"A misanthrope?" Jane asked.

"Not really. I don't think he hated anyone. He was simply too shy and timid to want to talk to strangers."

"How do you know this?"

"Both his boss and his sister, who were virtually the only people he felt comfortable speaking to, said so and clearly meant it. So far nobody but the local cop on the beat even knew who he was. And he'd seldom even seen Sven. Officer Jones would drop in to check on Sven's sister, who lost both her lower legs to diabetes."

"Oh, how awful for her. How will she manage without her brother?"

"It's a problem they're going to have to deal with, especially if he doesn't survive. But you'll understand better when I get to the end of this story."

"So what happened to Sven?"

"He came back the next morning, and as he was unloading his cleaning supplies from the back of his truck, he was struck hard on the side of his head."

"Did he see who did it?"

"No, probably not. By the time he was found, he was in a coma. He still is. That's why I called on his sister, to learn more about him. I asked if I could see his bedroom, thinking that bedrooms often tell you about a person's interests. Some, like you, have more books than anyone I know. I am, as you've seen, a slob who has never made his own bed."

"What was Sven's room like?"

The salads arrived, and after eating a few bites and pronouncing it a great dressing, but on too much lettuce, Mel went on, "Sven's room was neat and tidy. The house must have been where both Sven and his sister, Hilda, grew up. Nothing had changed since the 1970s, when Sven's parents put cowboy wallpaper up. You could have bounced a dime off the bed, it was so well made. A really huge, dreary, mostly brown jigsaw puzzle was set up near the window."

He took a few more bites of the salad as Jane was eating hers.

"I looked in his closet. Closets tell you things, too. Terribly neat. The whole bottom was filled with puzzle boxes, and on the back of the door was one of those pocket things for shoes. He had at least a dozen. One pair of loafers looked as if it had never been worn. So I pulled a shoe out and a neat roll of one-hundred-dollar bills with a rubber band around it fell out."

Jane gasped. "Blackmail! Remember I mentioned that as possible motive for trying to kill a janitor?"

"I'd given it some thought as well," Mel admitted. "But I don't believe he had the courage to blackmail strangers. You have to be very brazen and talk scary. 'I'll come after your family if you don't come up with the money' and so forth. It's also dangerous being a blackmailer. You don't know when your victim will meet you with a mob of cops hidden behind cars and vans. From hearing what his boss and his sister said, he simply couldn't have faced any stranger and been forceful and tough."

"You're really convinced about this," Jane said. She wasn't questioning his judgment. She knew it was a result of his experience and skills.

"Yes. But, Jane, when I came back with a warrant to search legally, the total hidden in his room was more than a hundred thousand dollars."

Jane lost her grip on her salad fork, which flipped over and fell on the floor. A waiter instantly replaced it.

Jane, embarrassed, thanked the waiter and, when he was gone, asked, "Did his sister know about the money?"

Mel nodded. "Apparently some, perhaps a lot, of the money is hers. While I was snooping before I got the warrant to search, she was chatting with Officer Jones, the cop who checks on her from time to time. She's considerably older than her brother and for a long time had a very well-paying job. When she had to leave because of the problems with her legs, she had a lot of pension money built up that's still being paid. She had also received disability payments from social security."

Jane put down her fork. "But even if

that's true, I don't think that between her pension, social security, and whatever her brother makes as a janitor, they could save that much money. Could they? They must have had expenses like everyone else. Property tax, food, utilities like water, gas, and electricity. And old houses often need new gutters, roofs, and furnaces. Why are you grinning like that? Aren't I making sense?"

"Are you finished with your salads?" The waiter was back.

"I think we are," Mel said. Jane nodded.

Then she said, "I hate getting this story in installments. Talk faster before the steaks get here or save it for later."

"I can sum it up in one word. Gambling."

"Gambling? Who?"

"Sven, of course. Every weekend."

"But you can't be solitary when you're in a casino. I've been in several and they were mobbed."

"Mobbed maybe. Especially on weekends, I'd imagine. But you don't have to talk to anyone if you don't want to."

The vigilant waiter saw the opportunity to bring their steaks and baked potatoes while Jane was sitting back considering this scenario.

They both applied themselves to the main course without talking much. Jane had ordered the largest filet mignon, done medium rare, and was planning to take home half of it to slice really thin and use on a sandwich the next day. Mel went through his entire T-bone. After the waiter had boxed up half of Jane's steak, Mel said, "Order yourself a dessert; I think I'll just have strong coffee. I want to finish this story and see what you think of it."

"I see already why you didn't explain what would happen to Sven's sister if he died," Jane said. "She'd own a house, inherit the whole amount of money, and be able to take a room or two, even her own wing, maybe, at a good nursing home."

When the waiter returned, Jane ordered a fudgy dark chocolate dessert, with coffee. She intended to take most of the dessert home as well. This restaurant wrapped up the leftovers in such pretty little boxes, tied up in ribbons, and she wanted to keep two of them.

While she nibbled at the dessert, Mel went on, "Sven liked to finish his cleaning jobs at the crack of dawn on Fridays so he could go to casinos in Iowa, St. Louis, or even Minneapolis. Then catch up with janitoring late on Sunday nights. A lot of driving time getting to and from the far-thest ones. But apparently profitable enough."

"And you believe this?"

"We circulated his picture from his driver's license to several of the casinos, and it seems to be true. Several of the cashiers recognized him. The employees and those monitoring the tables and slot machines on hidden cameras are really vig-ilant."

"He's either very lucky or cheating, to accumulate that much money," Jane said.

"Some people are always lucky. And he might have been lucky for a great many years, Janey. He might have been doing this most of his adult life."

"Where is the money now?"

"I stood over three cops, acting as vigi-lant as the casino employees, counting it out in thousands. And then I had an ar-mored truck take it to a safety-deposit box. My name and Hilda's are on the box. I left her a thousand dollars to get along on until, and if, her brother recovers.

"I wanted the whole neighborhood to know that the cash, which they didn't even know about, is gone," he went on. "And I have my men watching the house day and night, just in case somebody who was counting the bills told some friend about all that money over a boozy evening with his fellow officers. These were young cops counting the money. I hardly knew any of them very well. And I know the young ones sometimes can't resist gossiping with friends about interesting things they've done when they're sitting around in a bar."

Mel gave both the waiter and the maître d' generous tips.

As they were walking back to the car, Mel feeling really silly carrying two little packages tied up with pink ribbons, Jane asked, "Do either Sven or Hilda have children to pass this money to when they're both gone?"

"Neither ever married. At least Hilda Turner says so. It would be easy to check, and I think she's smart enough to know that and not lie about it," Mel said, opening the passenger door of his red MG and handing the cutesy boxes of leftovers to Jane.

"Then who gets all that money when both of them are gone?"

"I'm wondering about that, too. I'm assuming that Sven wanted to accumulate lots of money for his sister's care if her health deteriorated to the point that he couldn't keep her at home. It's just a theory, though."

"It's a nice theory," she said, leaning over to give him a kiss on the cheek. "You have to be a cynic to do your job so well. But you can't hide your kindly personality from me."

Mel was glad it was dark in the car. He was desperately afraid he might — heaven forfend — be blushing.

"It's just one theory, Jane," he said somewhat gruffly. "They might have earmarked this money for some charity. Or set up some kind of trust to help indigent jigsaw puzzle fanatics."

Mel put the car in gear and turned on the headlights. "Your place or mine?"

"I'd love to go to yours, but it's nearly eleven. I want to be sure the kids are all home. And I have to be up early to feed them before Mike goes to work and Katie goes to summer school."

"They can't do toast and eggs?"

"They could, but they won't and will be starving by ten and blame me. Besides, I have to get ready to hit the grocery store and put things away before the needlepoint class."

"You're still enjoying that? Why haven't you shown me your project?"

"I will when it's done."

Mel walked to her front door and gave her one of those kisses that turned Jane into jelly.

Chapter Eighteen

Mel was in his office early Tuesday morning, going through the rest of the paperwork regarding the death of Denny Roth and other files on the attack on Sven Turner. It always astonished and dismayed him in cases like this how much paperwork crimes generated, as well as how slowly some of the data he'd asked for finally trickled in.

There was a new report on his desk that was interesting but not very enlightening. Sven's doctor had called in while he was having dinner with Jane, and left a message that while Sven was still only semiconscious, he was occasionally moving around, apparently trying to run from something. He was also mumbling something. Opinions on what he was trying to say varied. Something like "rabbit" or "ratchet." Or maybe "catch it." This might or might not mean he'd ever get better.

His sister, Hilda, was also eager to visit him, which the doctor approved of, if the police would allow it, and if she could find someone to bring her to the hospital. Perhaps Detective VanDyne could prevail on social services to arrange it if he approved her visiting.

Mel immediately called back. Naturally, the doctor wasn't available. Mel left a message that he had received the physician's message and agreed that it would be a good idea if Mr. Turner's sister visited and that he'd arrange for it. There was a chance, however remote, that she might understand what her brother was trying to say.

Social services would want a lot of paperwork filled out before they could get her to the hospital. And they'd have to arrange for a van with a lift for her wheelchair. Mel told the man he spoke to that he'd authorize Officer Jones, who knew her best, to come and get the forms to Sven's sister and return them.

That would generate at least fifteen or twenty more pieces of paperwork in triplicate for everyone to file.

But Officer Jones said, "I could borrow my aunt's van. Her late husband was in a wheelchair and it's equipped with a mechanical ramp. She never even drives it anymore. She's got herself a little Honda."

"Officer Jones, have you any idea how much time, trouble, and paperwork this has saved? Are you sure you want to do this?"

"Nobody uses the van anymore. I like Old Lady Turner, and will be glad to fetch her and bring her home."

"You're a good man. Thank you. And I wonder if — I shouldn't even ask this, but I will. If there's any way you can find out what they intend to do with all that money, I'd like to know."

"I'll do my best to think of a way to bring it up," he said. "She likes talking to me. Is it important?"

"Frankly, no," Mel admitted. "It's sheer curiosity. Don't bother if you don't feel comfortable about this."

"I'm curious, too."

Mel said, "I'll call the hospital back and tell them you're bringing her to visit her brother. Be sure to go in with her and see if you can decipher what Sven is trying to say."

"He's talking?"

"Not exactly. He's about half conscious and trying to say something. Nobody can tell what it is. Maybe his sister will understand him better than strangers."

Mel decided he should also be there at the meeting of brother and sister. But only in the background. He was casually loitering in the hall outside Sven's room when Officer Jones wheeled Miss Turner out of the elevator. She greeted Mel politely. "Thank you, Detective VanDyne, for making this possible."

He smiled and nodded and followed them into the room.

"Wheel me as close as you can," she said to Officer Jones.

When she was close enough, she put her hand on her brother's forearm and said, "Sven, I'm here. Hilda is here. And I'm going to see to it that you don't lollygag around in this bed for much longer. Sven, open your eyes and look at me."

He turned his head toward her, his eyes opening slightly, a bit cross-eyed.

"That's better," Hilda Turner said firmly, and patted his arm rather roughly.

Mel and Officer Jones exchanged looks that said, *She's a tougher lady than we knew.* Mel realized that it was probably she, as the big sister, who had bossed Sven around since childhood, and he was accustomed to obeying her.

"You're going to get much better with me around, Sven. If nice Officer Jones can bring me here every day, or even every other day, I'm going to see that you come home soon, good as new. Do you understand me?"

Sven, confined by tubes and monitors,

managed a slight nod.

"All right. Now tell me this word you've been saying over and over," Hilda said in a firm voice.

"Rabbit."

The nurses, the doctor, and everyone else in the crowded room clearly understood it this time.

"Rabbit?" Hilda asked. "What does that mean?"

"Rabbit!" he repeated loudly, then closed his eyes again and took a deep breath after this effort.

"Sven, take a nice nap," his sister said, pressing a freshly ironed handkerchief to her eyes. "I'll be back soon. You *are* going to recover."

She looked up at Officer Jones, and he turned her wheelchair around gingerly so as to not run over anybody's feet or some tubing or pull the plug out of some important bit of medical equipment. Mel held the door open and followed them.

"You're a courageous woman, Miss Turner," Mel said. "And I suspect you, and only you, can make him recover."

"Would you like to go down to the lunchroom and have a cup of coffee or tea?" Officer Jones asked Miss Turner.

Her voice was now a bit shaky as she

said, "That would be very kind of you. He looked so awful with all those tubes and beeping machines. But he sat with me in this same hospital when I lost my lower legs. He must have been as worried then about me as I am about him now."

Officer Jones got her settled and went to fetch flavored but unsweetened tea for Miss Turner and coffee for himself and Mel.

Hilda Turner was getting a better grip on herself and confided in Mel, "I can hardly believe that I forgot something important. There's a corridor between this hospital and some small apartments for the families of seriously ill patients. That's where Sven stayed when I was in here. Do you think I could stay there and save Officer Jones the trouble of hauling me here and back home every day?"

Mel said, "I'll find out."

"It's not that I can't afford it," she said with a faint smile.

Mel thought this was a good time to ask what they intended to do with all their money, but couldn't bring himself to do so when she was so worried.

Instead he asked, "What do you think 'rabbit' means to him? He said it so clearly."

"I have no idea. There's something tickling the back of my mind, but I can't quite grasp it."

"You'll let me know when you do, won't you?"

"It's probably something really trivial. I will tell you, if I can figure out why he'd say it. And, Detective, when you contact the manager of those apartments, would you explain I need one with bars to hold on to in the bathroom?"

When Officer Jones returned, carefully carrying their drinks on a flimsy tray, Mel explained what they'd been talking about while he was gone.

"Apartments for families? Who would have guessed? But I don't mind driving you every day, Miss Turner, if Detective VanDyne approves it. And my aunt, as I told you, never wants to drive it again."

"I can't put you to all that trouble," she said, once more becoming the big sister and bossy. "But I will have to be taken home and ask my neighbor to pack my clothing and medicines — if Detective VanDyne can get me an apartment."

"I'll use whatever clout it takes to see that you have one," Mel said.

"I could do your packing," Officer Jones said.

She said, almost sounding girlish, "You? Packing up my underwear? I don't think so."

Officer Jones turned slightly pink. "Oh."

After Mel had reserved an apartment adjoining the hospital that met Miss Turner's needs and Officer Jones had her on her way home to be helped to pack by her neighbor, Mel returned to his office to start over with his stacks of paperwork that both the death of Denny and the attack on Sven had generated. He'd already put what he'd gone through in three piles on the counter behind his desk.

The first pile was papers that were entirely irrelevant. This was the smallest pile. The second consisted of documents and copies of interviews that he suspected might not be worthwhile, but which he'd go through again. Papers that he believed might contain the key to either or both of the crimes made up the largest pile. And he still had a big mass of folders and loose papers remaining that would end up in one of the piles.

When he'd made significant headway, he went around the corner and bought a sandwich, chips, and a soda to eat a late lunch at his desk. Then he called Jane.

"Did you learn any more about anything useful at your needlepoint class this morning?"

"Tazz didn't show up, thank goodness. I think I really scared her away."

"She deserved being scared away."

"I just wish I could scare Elizabeth away."

"Who is Elizabeth?"

"One of the other people in the needlepointing class. She's such a snoop. She mentioned to Ms. Bunting that she's seen Ms. Bunting's husband drop her off and wanted to know what he did while she was in class. As if it were any of her business. Ms. Bunting said he was going to the country club where he'd played golf earlier. He'd lost his driver."

"What driver? He has somebody who drives him around?"

"No, it's an old-fashioned name for a golf club, Ms. Bunting said. Like mashies, wedgies, spoons, lofters, niblicks, and something called cleek, that might have been a club or a brand of club. Ms. Bunting wasn't sure which," Jane said.

"Elizabeth tried to correct her," Jane went on, "and tell her that golf clubs had numbers, not names. Ms. Bunting did a royal 'putting down,' saying that the clubs were her husband's father's. Antiques. Very valuable, and designated by the names they were called when they were made."

"Sounds like this Elizabeth needs to take a few lessons in etiquette," Mel said.

"She's Junior League. She's expected to be polite. I guess nobody told her that when she signed up."

Mel shifted the subject, not much caring about Elizabeth's manners. "I have a little news for you. Officer Jones took Miss Turner to see her brother, and the visit really perked him up. She did the firm 'big sister' act, telling him to pull himself together. And it started to work."

"He's fully conscious, then?"

"No, but he opened his eyes for a brief moment and clearly said 'rabbit' so that it was understandable to everyone in the room. Not that it's revealed anything useful. His sister didn't know what he meant by it either. If anyone can bring him out of it, it's his sister. She's a much firmer, more determined woman than I imagined. Does 'rabbit' suggest anything to you?"

"I've never met or even seen the man. How would I know? My only guess, off the top of my head, is that he caught a glimpse of his attacker and only remembered that he had big yellowish teeth."

Mel laughed. "That's a big stretch of your imagination, Janey."

"Well, you asked and it could be true. Are you certain that these two crimes were done by the same person?"

"Not certain. But my gut instinct tells me they probably were. I just wanted to check in with you. Now I have to wade through the rest of my eighteen pounds of paperwork."

"Did you really weigh it?" Jane asked with a laugh.

"I just estimated."

Chapter Nineteen

Mel worked late Tuesday evening. He was determined to get through all the piles of paperwork he'd sorted. When it was done, he went to McDonald's for a burger and fries. Since the food wasn't interesting, merely filling, he let his mind wander over what he knew. He was as certain as he could be that the death of Denny Roth and the attack on Sven Turner were related.

Sven had called his boss that night and said he'd do the theater early in the morning because he heard people talking inside. Maybe he had recognized the voices. Maybe he knew who both were. Was the other one "rabbit"?

Maybe Sven had even heard the sound of something crashing. The blow that killed Denny Roth.

But there was no point in waiting for Sven to come fully to his senses. He might never remember, nor be able to speak clearly enough to be understood except for that one word he'd gathered all his strength to say repeatedly.

Mel needed desperately to know more

about Denny and still couldn't reach his parents. The local officer was getting as tired of checking their house as Mel was of perpetually trying to reach them by phone. Often the victim of a crime was the key to who perpetrated it. But Denny, so far, was a cipher. Maybe something would turn up soon that would be helpful. Some old bitter enemy who had tracked Denny down in Chicago, perhaps.

His only suspect was Professor Imry. And Mel couldn't convince himself that Imry was guilty. He was sly, ambitious, and tactless. Not a likeable person. But that didn't mean he was a killer who could go haywire over someone correcting his grammar.

Mel wouldn't have minded suspecting John Bunting, even though there was no reason to. He was a drunk and a lech. He'd also based his lifelong career on the skills of his wife. Without her, he'd have been nothing.

A man of his age who ignored his only daughter and his grandchildren was slime. It would be a joy to put him away for good. And probably a relief to his wife. Ms. Bunting had been chained to him her whole adult life, having to support him by her own talent and hard work, he suspected.

He sat up straighter. Why not give his interviews with Bunting's old friends a quick review?

The men he'd spoken to about Bunting's alibi really had very little to say about him. They were clearly more in touch with each other and only saw him infrequently, on the rare occasions when he visited Chicago. None of them had much in common with him except the schools they'd gone to so many decades ago. Perhaps they merely put up with him when he wanted to get together with them.

He riffled through his paperwork on the telephone interviews he'd had with each of them. He was right. They talked about each other. Nobody had much to say about Bunting himself, except that they'd played golf with him one day, with a lunch afterward, and had a dinner with him as well.

It was Mel's own fault that he hadn't asked the right questions. The old boys were interesting and he'd let them off too easily. Because they were so old? No. None of them, however feeble in body, had seemed to have lost their wits and ambitions.

He'd interview them again, focusing on what they really thought about the actor. It might be useless. Or it might not be.

Bunting wasn't a good man. Maybe he was a worse man than Mel knew. Or maybe not.

Of all the old friends of Bunting's he'd interviewed before, the canniest was the attorney who was still going into the office, meddling. He'd succinctly answered the questions Mel asked and hadn't volunteered a single extra word.

Mel would make an appointment in the morning to see him in the office he still maintained.

The lawyer, Irving Walsh, welcomed him to his office Wednesday morning and asked a secretary to bring along coffee. "Do you mind if I smoke a cigar while we talk? I'll open a window if you wish."

"I like the smell of a good cigar, but have never smoked one. Please go ahead," Mel replied. He really hated the smell of cigars but wanted Walsh to be relaxed and content to talk.

When the secretary had left the coffee, a brand as expensive as the cigar, Mr. Walsh said, "We've spoken before, but on the phone. What more do you want to know?"

"There was a question I asked everyone else and neglected to ask you. After the dinner with your old friends and John

Bunting, did you all leave the establishment together?"

Walsh picked up a silver-plated pen knife to cut the end off his cigar. When it was lighted and he had politely opened a window and turned on a small fan blowing toward the window, he said, "As a matter of fact, we didn't. John Bunting left early. He said his wife was waiting up for him and made a feeble joke about what a tight rein she kept on him."

"Did you happen to notice the time he left?"

"About an hour or forty-five minutes before the rest of us called it a night. Maybe about ten or a little earlier. I'd told my driver to pick me up at eleven."

"Are you certain of this?"

"Why wouldn't I be?"

"Because I asked the rest of the group you were with, and every one of them said you'd all left together and chatted on the sidewalk as your drivers arrived."

"They all had far more to drink than I did," Walsh said, fiddling with the growing ash on his cigar. "I haven't had a single glass of anything alcoholic for years. Maybe they really thought he was still with us."

"Perhaps," Mel said. "Do you like John Bunting?"

"Why do you ask?"

"It's my job to ask nosy questions."

Walsh smiled. "So was it my job at one time. I'm still in the habit. No, I don't like him. The rest of us had the benefit of a good education and, I admit, family ties that helped us out. John has ridden on his wife's coattails, so to speak, for his entire adult life. If it weren't for her charm, talent, and hard work, he'd be out of work and broke. Or even dead by now. And unlike the rest of us, he never talks about his daughter or grandchildren. He seems to have no interest in them."

"That's my impression as well, and the opinion of a friend of mine who knows them slightly," Mel admitted. "Do the rest of your old friends feel the same way about him?"

"Most of them. Except for Ed Kowalski. He and Bunting were always in touch. Even in college, they stuck together. I suspected, but won't go on the record, that Ed was supplying Bunting with drugs from his dad's pharmacy. It might have just been vitamins, but they were so furtive about it that it made me wonder if it was something stronger."

"Do you think Kowalski still does this?"

Walsh nodded. "I'll deny I said this if

this comes to court, but Ed passed a bottle of something to Bunting the night we got together. They were sitting next to each other, but I was on the other side of Ed and saw it changing hands."

"Thank you," Mel said. "And I'll try to use this, if I need to, without using your name."

"That will be tricky."

"It will. But I might not be required to use the information. Or you might like to testify if we need you to."

Walsh simply raised his eyebrows and took another puff of his cigar.

When Mel returned to his office to make more detailed notes of his discussion with Irving Walsh, he had a message to call Hilda Turner at his convenience. He did so when he'd completed his notes.

"This is, I admit, rather silly, Detective VanDyne," she said. "I've thought and thought about Sven saying 'rabbit' and I think I might know why."

"Could you explain?"

Miss Turner sighed. "It's probably not going to help the least bit. Are you a father?"

"Not yet. Probably not ever," Mel said with a smile in his voice.

"Me too, not a mother," she replied, laughing. "Well, here is what I've remembered and it most likely means nothing. In the old days, mothers who had babies as winter approached used to make or buy these little pillowcase sort of bags. They were to keep the baby warm in a cold winter wind. There were a couple of buttons on each side and a sort of hood to put lightly over the baby's head to keep him or her warm."

"I think I grasp the concept. But where does a rabbit come into it?"

"Sven was a really little baby. Hardly more than five pounds, and he came home from the hospital with a cold. So my mother made him a rabbit-skin sack, lined with wool. He never had another cold and grew fast. Pretty soon he was too big to fit in it, and it was summer. But he wouldn't part with it. Wouldn't go to sleep without it in his crib. When he was almost six and had rubbed off all the fur by then, he gave it up. So it's simply a comforting memory. He must have been dreaming about one of his favorite things in childhood."

"He certainly didn't sound comfortable when he said it," Mel replied.

"That's because he was trying so hard to say it right. Don't you think that's why?"

"It's possible, I suppose. Well, this probably isn't relevant to the case, but it is interesting. I don't think I've ever seen or heard of such a thing. But thank you for letting me know."

Mel hung up the phone, still smiling, and tidied up the rest of his files. Half an hour later, he felt he had everything sorted properly and dialed Jane.

When she answered, he said, "I've learned one thing about Sven and his saying 'rabbit' so forcefully."

Jane said, "It must be important. You sound so cheerful."

"No, I'm cheerful because it's completely irrelevant but kind of a funny story." He parroted what Miss Turner had explained.

"Oh, I know what those are. My grandmother used to make one for every single baby due to be born close to winter. But not with rabbit fur, that I remember. She made them of soft flannel in several layers, the best color on the outside. Pretty soon, women from neighboring towns started asking her to make them for their own upcoming babies. She eventually made good money on them, and finally found a catalog that sold a pretty plaid flannel in shades of light blue, light green, light pink, and light yellow."

Jane thought for a second and said, "I think I still have one of them stashed away somewhere that she hadn't quite finished when she died. I'll try to find it to show you."

"Is this the grandmother who grew the bing cherries?"

"It is. She called the flannel bags baby buntings." She was silent for a moment and repeated, "Buntings."

"Bunting," Mel said. He was no longer cheerful.

Jane said, "Don't get carried away, Mel. It's sheer coincidence."

"Maybe not. The theater had lots of those brochures showing pictures and bios of the actors all over the place. They'd probably been printed well ahead of time. It's possible Sven couldn't quite remember the name and substituted something close to it. Something hauled up in his subconscious from his childhood."

"I know you probably dislike John Bunting as much as most of the cast does, but that doesn't matter."

"Whether I like him or not isn't the point. I have to consider this as a possibility, though."

Chapter Twenty

Mel turned up at the rehearsal that evening. It was a technical walk-through, he was told. He didn't ask what that meant. It was quite obvious. It mostly involved final lighting decisions. The actors walked through, saying their lines. Not with much feeling, apparently, and certain lights shifted with the action as they moved around the set.

One scene seemed to be causing trouble. "That dress is an unattractive color," the lighting expert from the college called down to the stage. "I've tried all my filters and nothing helps. Tazz, do you have a different dress we could use for this scene? Blue or green would be better than the violent red."

Everything came to a halt while the lighting expert, Tazz, Imry, and Joani consulted.

Mel slipped around the back, searching for John Bunting. He found him outside the stage door, smoking a cigarette.

"You a smoker?" Bunting asked, fishing in his jacket pocket.

"I used to be," Mel replied. "Go ahead

with yours. I hear you lost a valuable golf club."

Bunting must have inhaled too fast and had a fit of coughing. "How did you hear that?" he finally managed to ask.

"I'm friends with Mrs. Jeffry, and your wife mentioned it at the needlepoint meeting."

"Friends, huh? She's a tasty-looking woman. Doesn't her husband mind?"

Mel wanted to punch him, but said mildly, "She's a widow. Her husband died in a car accident many years ago. What kind of golf club was this?"

"Why do you ask? Are you a golfer?"

"Yes, but not a good one," Mel said with a disarming smile.

"It was my best driver. Inherited the whole set from my father. Nice heft. Just the right length. He bought the set in Scotland in 1912."

"Would you like me to ask around to see if I can find out what became of it?" Mel offered, as if speaking offhandedly.

"Why would you care?"

Mel shrugged. "I'm a detective. I have lots of connections. How do you think you lost it?"

Bunting was still a bit suspicious of this interest, but said, "All my boarding school pals and I played at our favorite course early in our visit. Then we went to lunch. We left all our golf bags in the storage area. Apparently somebody ran into them and they all fell over. I assumed, when I first missed it, that whoever did it put mine back in the wrong bag. I've called all the men I was with to see if my driver was accidentally put into their bags, but they all checked, and it wasn't."

"I can see how that could happen, especially if it was someone who didn't know much about sets of clubs."

"Those minor employees at places like this are all foreigners these days," Bunting complained. "None of them have a brain in their heads."

Mel had to paste a fake smile on his face. "If you could describe it, I could ask around. It's probably in a secondhand store by now."

"No, thanks. I'll hunt for it myself."

"Suit yourself. Listen, I think I hear someone calling you," Mel lied.

Bunting went back inside. Mel walked away from the door and down the alley behind the theater and took out his cell phone. He called his office assistant, giving what the assistant probably thought were very odd instructions to do searches. And what to do with the evidence if it was located.

He went back into the theater, looking for Jane. He found her sitting in the front row of seats, needlepointing. She had something weird on her head, like glasses with little flashlights at each side.

"That's cute," he said.

"It isn't cute at all," she said with a laugh. "But it lets me see what I'm doing. Why are you here tonight?"

"Just snooping around again. Have the caterers come yet?"

"They should be here any moment. Shelley just went to look for them in the alley. Good ones are getting thin on the ground. She's still hoping to find at least two that are really good, and is only pleased with one so far."

A few minutes later they saw Shelley at the edge of the stage, telling everyone that the snack supper would be ready in ten minutes.

"Are you going to be a taster along with me?" Jane asked.

"I will. I haven't had dinner. I might stick around and eat all the leftovers."

"I have plenty of good leftovers at home," Jane said, taking off her headgear and bundling up her needlepoint project.

"I planned to have them with the kids when I get home. Want to join us?"

"I'll be a taster and eat again with you later. I'm really hungry."

"How's the investigation into Denny's death going?" Jane asked as they strolled toward the side steps to the stage.

"Fits and starts. No solid evidence yet."

"And you still can't get an answer from Denny's parents?"

"Nope. And I'm driving the local cops crazy, checking to see if anyone is finally at home. I hope I never have to meet them in person. They'd probably want to beat me senseless. I wouldn't blame them."

Shelley agreed to Mel tasting the snacks, and soon after eating, he and Jane left the theater in separate cars. When they arrived within moments of each other at Jane's house, her kids were already tucking into the leftovers. Mike had made a huge sandwich with a thick slice of meatloaf, mayo, and tomato. Todd had made a more modest sandwich with a thin slice of meatloaf and no tomato. He claimed that tomatoes gave him spots. Katie had picked at a tuna salad Jane had made before leaving for the theater. There was plenty of everything left for Mel.

Jane had seldom seen Mel eat so much

at one time. He restrained himself from gulping it down, but ate steadily, complimenting Jane as he finished off the last of the tuna salad. "Do you have any dessert?" he asked.

"Only York peppermint patties."

"One will do."

They left the kids to clean up what was still left, and went to sit in the living room.

"I feel like one of your cats who just consumed a muskrat. But unlike them, I won't throw up on the sofa or the patio," Mel said. "I don't remember ever being as hungry as I was tonight. I can't be sure, but I don't think I had anything to eat all day except a small bag of potato chips."

Jane turned the television on to a music station playing light classical and said, "A long day for you, then? Have you learned anything else?"

"No, but I'm close now. Those Roth people are bound to come home sometime, and I have some other searches going on."

His cell phone rang, and he stood up with an overstuffed groan and fished in his trouser pocket. "VanDyne here — yes!" He paused to listen for a while. "Good. Arriving when? Thanks for going to so much trouble to help us."

He turned off the phone and subsided

on the sofa. "I ate too much. I feel as if I've turned into the Michelin Man."

"That sounded important."

"The well-traveled Roths finally came home. They're on a plane to Chicago as we speak. I'll have to meet them at their hotel at ten-thirty. Meanwhile, I need to walk this meal off."

"Let me know what you find out, if you can," Jane asked as Mel practically fled to his car.

"Who was that man who just ran through our kitchen?" Mike called out to his mother.

Mel went back to his office and did some research on the Internet before going to meet the Roths. He was standing at the door of their hotel, holding a sign that said "Roth," when a taxi pulled up and unloaded a ton of luggage. An excruciatingly thin middle-aged woman emerged and said harshly, "Who are you?"

"I'm Detective VanDyne. I'm in charge of your son's case. Your room is confirmed. You don't need to check in and your luggage will be delivered."

"Who killed him, and why?" she demanded.

"We're not sure yet. I'm sorry for your

loss, ma'am. I know you've had a very long, hard day, I'll take you or your husband to officially identify him first thing in the morning, and then we'll have to talk about him."

"I can't imagine why we weren't told sooner. My aunt in Portland, Oregon, had our schedule with telephone numbers, and my brother in Nebraska had them, too."

Mel was dumbfounded by this remark, but merely said, "Mrs. Roth, we didn't know you had an aunt in Oregon or a brother in Nebraska. How could we have reached them? I made several calls a day and your answering machine refused to record them. Is that all of your luggage?"

Her husband approached, lugging some of the bags. Mel introduced himself again and said, repeating himself, "I'm very sorry for your loss, Mr. Roth. I know you've had a long day. Unfortunately, I'll need one or both of you to identify your son in the morning and then be interviewed."

The man, his eyes red and downcast, said quietly, "Yes. I see. What time in the morning?"

"Let's say ten o'clock?" Mel suggested. "I'll meet you right here. I'm sincerely sorry that you have to go through this, and will try to make this as easy on you as I'm able."

He had to tip the taxi driver, who was still standing by his vehicle with the trunk open. And then Mel tipped the valet who was loading up the luggage. Mel seldom let himself make snap judgments, but it was clear that Mrs. Roth was a type of woman he'd met before. An angry woman. One of those women who wanted full control of the lives of her family. And when she and women like her lost that control, they placed the blame on someone — almost anyone — who crossed their paths. Mrs. Roth was angry that the police hadn't solved the murder of her son. She was angry at Mel in particular. She was probably mad at her husband for no reason. Mel wasn't looking forward to dealing with her tomorrow. He wished he could deal with her husband, who was obviously grieving. He was more likely to want to talk about his son.

Chapter Twenty-one

The needlepoint group was really making progress. Sam had taken out all his sections that were too tight and redone them. Shelley's sampler was more than halfway done and looked gorgeous. Jane was only slightly behind Shelley. Jane, like Sam, had been forced to remove one section that hadn't worked out, and discovered that it was harder to work with canvas that was slightly limp from already being used. Jane and Sam sympathized with each other over this unpleasant surprise.

"Next time I do a sampler, I'll remember to do it right to begin with," Jane said.

"I hope I will, too," Sam agreed.

Again, Tazz hadn't turned up, which was a relief to Jane. She wondered whether Tazz was embarrassed or furious or both that Jane had bluntly turned down the idea of writing Tazz's costume book for her. Or maybe Tazz's absence had nothing to do with Jane.

Elizabeth, who apparently had more time than most of the group to work on her sampler, had only four sections to finish. Jane was still doubtful about Elizabeth's choices of colors, but apparently Elizabeth had an eye for contrasts that really did look good.

After they had all complimented each other, Elizabeth asked Ms. Bunting what her husband was doing today while Ms. Bunting was at the meeting.

"The old fool is looking for his missing golf club at secondhand stores," she said with a laugh. "Nobody but an idiot, or a rich person wanting a receipt for an antique to reduce his taxes, would turn it over to a secondhand store. If I were looking for it, I'd go to pawnshops. Or order a duplicate on eBay."

"What's eBay?" Elizabeth asked.

The rest of them looked at her with astonishment. "It's a place on the Internet that holds thousands of auctions," Shelley said.

"There are also lots of golf club sites in other places on the Internet," Sam put in. "Some sell restored antique golf clubs. My son-in-law is an avid collector of them. It makes it really easy to buy him birthday and Christmas presents."

"What will we do when we're all through with our samplers?" Elizabeth asked Martha, clearly not interested in the subject at hand. She had no interest in the Internet. Jane suspected that Elizabeth had never, and probably never would, own or operate a computer. And was undoubtedly proud of herself for it.

"We're going to master basket-weave patterns," Martha said. "I've noticed that none of you seem to have used this valuable stitch. It's the most durable of all of them. We'll be making a pillow, blocking it, adding special stitches around the edging, mastering trim for the surround, and stuffing the pillow properly when that's done. If you want to take the second level of classes later, those deal with creating your own designs. Mazes, animals, Christmas stockings, using beading and ornaments."

Shelley's eyes lit up like beacons. "I can't wait to take that class."

Only Jane knew of Shelley's vast collection of pretty beads, little buttons, and tiny ornaments. Shelley never had figured out what to do with them. Now she knew.

The worst part of Mel's job used to be taking people to the morgue to identify their nearest and dearest. For one thing, it was fiercely cold there and stank of formaldehyde and antiseptic. Thank goodness, eight years ago they'd changed this. Now the body, with only the face showing, was wheeled into a room with a glass partition. No odor. No hint of the stem-to-stern autopsy. There was a curtain behind the glass that would open when the people responsible for identifying the body were in place.

Still, it was shocking.

When the curtain opened, Mr. Roth looked as if he was about to faint. Mel led him to a chair nearby. "I'm sorry I have to ask, but is this your son?"

Mr. Roth had bent forward, hands over his eyes, and was trying gulp back his urge to cry.

"Of course it's our son," Mrs. Roth said. "Harry, get a grip. We have to face up to this."

As if Harry had to be told this, Mel thought.

Mrs. Roth frowned at Mel and demanded, "Close those curtains. We've seen enough."

"Come along when you're both ready," Mel told them. "I'll be waiting in the hall for you. There are questions I need to ask. Take all the time you need."

Mel sat down by the door, simmering. He should try to see this from Mrs. Roth's viewpoint. She'd lost her only child. But why did she have to be so rude? Not only to him, but to her husband.

He only had to sit there for a few minutes before the couple emerged.

Mrs. Roth was pale, but composed. Mr. Roth was still mopping at his eyes.

"I'm taking you to my office in an unmarked police car. You'll be more comfortable there," Mel said. "I'd like to interview you and find out what your son was like." As they entered the elevator, Mel added, "I'd like to speak to each of you separately. Mrs. Roth, could I order you some coffee or tea while you wait?"

"I'm not waiting. We'll be interviewed together."

"I'm sorry, but you will have to wait," Mel said firmly.

"Then orange pekoe tea with sugar," she snapped.

When she'd settled irritably in the outer office, Mel offered Mr. Roth coffee, which Roth accepted numbly. Mel waited for the man to speak.

"He was our only child — we adopted him," Mr. Roth said softly. "Aggie couldn't have children. I must apologize for her behavior. You mustn't think she doesn't care that Denny is dead. She's simply keeping her armor on — she's good at that."

He teared up again. "I loved the boy from the first. It was a little harder for Aggie. I think she thought adoption wasn't quite 'nice' and that it suggested something was wrong with her. It might have been better if we'd taken a little girl instead. But he was such a good boy. I taught him to play softball. I took him to circuses. I helped him with homework. I . . ."

He couldn't go on. Mel handed him a box of tissues and went to look out the window for a few moments until Roth said, "I'm sorry. What else do you want to know?"

"Did Denny make friends easily?"

"Of course. Aggie and I made sure of that. She did the room-mother things, made him take dancing lessons, which, surprisingly, he liked. She threw wonderful birthdays and let him invite all his friends. And he always had lots of them. He was happy until . . ."

"Until what?"

"Until he decided out of the blue that he wanted to know who his biological parents were. Aggie was appalled. He always knew he was adopted but never seemed to care until two years ago."

"Did it hurt your feelings?" Mel asked.

"Not especially. I suspected it might

happen when he grew up. I myself was adopted and had wonderful parents, and I never cared who actually sired me."

"Did you or your wife know who Denny's biological parents were?"

"No. The adoption agency offered to tell us the available adoptee's ethnic background. We didn't care."

"How did your wife take this idea of Denny's interest in finding his genetic parents?"

"She hated it. She felt that all that we had done for him had been wasted. She considered it a personal betrayal."

"Did your son have any enemies that you know of?"

"No. Until he got this bug in his ear about finding his 'real' parents, he had nothing but friends. It changed him. It became an obsession and he dropped all his friends to pursue it."

Mel's interview with Mrs. Roth didn't surprise him. First, she was outraged that she had to wait so long, "And the girl who served me tea never came back with the sugar I'd asked for."

So Mrs. Roth had also been rude to the young secretary who brought her tea, Mel thought.

"Well, it's time for your husband to sit around now. Tell me about Denny."

"He was such a nice boy. And we treated him as if he were a prince. He had everything he wanted. Good, expensive clothing, a generous allowance. We even bought him his first car when he turned sixteen and paid the taxes and registration fees for him."

"And then?"

"He took up with the idea of being an actor, of all things. I explained how hard it was to be an actor. All those interviews and classes, and the sort of competition there was. Every good-looking young person in the world wants to be an actor or actress. Very few of them succeed. But he wouldn't listen to me. He actually moved out of our home to stay in some dismal apartments. Can you imagine?"

"What did your husband think of this?" Mel asked.

"He stayed out of it, saying Denny was an adult and had to make his own decisions. And it just became worse."

"In what way?"

"He came home for a Thanksgiving dinner and told us he'd decided he wanted to find his 'real' parents. *'Real'* is the word he used. *We* were his real parents. We'd raised him from the day he was only two days old. I felt as if he'd stuck a knife in my chest."

"Did your husband agree?" Mel asked.

"No. He said the same stupid thing. Denny was entitled to do so, if it meant so much to him."

"Did Denny succeed in finding out anything?"

"I have no idea," she said. "And I don't want to know. If this is all you need to ask us, we need to get on with arranging the funeral. We have three plots in a cemetery here in Chicago we bought while we lived here. One for me, one for Harry, and one for Denny. Someday we'll be there with him again. And we need to know where his things are. His clothes, his books, his checkbook so we can cancel the account."

"They're in boxes. They'll be delivered to your hotel as soon as you want."

"Today," she said firmly, standing up and heading for the door. She stopped briefly, and said, "You *will* tell us who killed him when you get around to finding out, won't you?"

She didn't even wait for an answer — just slammed the door on her way out.

Mel was simply glad she was gone. During Mrs. Roth's rant, he'd had an insight that might prove worthwhile. He knew exactly which pile of paperwork it was in. The one that he thought he'd never need again. He went looking for it.

Chapter Twenty-two

When Jane and Shelley left the needlepoint shop, Shelley suggested they stop somewhere for lunch.

"We're on our last caterer tonight for the dress rehearsal and have to feed quite a lot of extra people. The whole cast and crew. Props people, lighting people, even the scene painters and their teacher will be there."

"Do you think you have caterers for tonight who can cope well?" Jane asked.

"Only if we do it in the lobby, which the college has approved. In fact, most caterers like to feed a real meal to a couple of hundred people rather than the snack suppers they've done so far. That's the real test of their skills."

"We haven't tried Chinese catering, so for lunch, let's go to that Chinese restaurant we always like," Jane suggested. "They have the best jasmine tea I've ever tasted."

When they'd placed their orders, Shelley said, "I went to that Internet site that you told me about. The Annie Silverstone one. She seems to be an attractive, interesting person with a good background in publishing. But there weren't the details I wanted to see."

"Like what?" Jane asked.

"Like who are the writers she represents? We know Felicity is one, but you'd think she'd mention others."

"I think most of her authors wouldn't want to be mentioned," Jane said. "It would invite people with crappy manuscripts to send them, claiming that someone like Felicity had recommended the agent. Even if Felicity had never heard of the person."

"Hmm. I hadn't thought of that," Shelley said. "I suppose it could even happen to you if you were to be listed on the site. You haven't heard from Ms. Silverstone yet, have you?"

"Not yet."

"I'm sure you'll hear from her soon."

"Things in publishing sometimes go very slowly, I think. Especially in August and December. And there are still two other agents who are the heads of their agencies and specialize in selling mysteries."

"Are you interested in seeing the whole dress rehearsal tonight?" Shelley asked.

"Not especially. But if you want to, I'll stick it out. I'd like to see how the costumes and sets look, if nothing else. You drive this time. I'm starving for spring rolls and you'll get us there sooner."

"But you already ordered them for lunch."

"So? What's your point?" Jane asked.

Mel's request to search pawnshops for old golf drivers paid off all too well. They had come in in droves. Eight of them at least. Three were clearly new. A waste of time. He took note of which officers had turned them in. The other five needed to be examined more closely. The more there were, the longer it was going to take. He looked them over and only sent three along to the experts.

If positive results didn't come in, there were two more he'd have to submit. All of them as per his instructions had been bagged and the searchers had tried to find out, as best they could, who had pawned them and where they'd found them.

Jane had eaten two whole appetizers — spring rolls and crab Rangoon, her favorites — and spicy orange-flavored Mongolian beef. Half of which she'd brought home. She'd also gone through four cups of jasmine tea. She stuffed the box with the leftovers in the fridge and nearly ran to the downstairs half-bath the moment she reached home. As she came out, the phone started ringing.

She glanced at the caller ID and saw that it was a New York City number.

"Is this Jane Jeffry?"

"Yes, this is she," Jane said breathlessly.

"I'm Annie Silverstone. Did I catch you at a bad time?"

Jane got a grip on herself and said, "Not at all. I've been hoping to hear from you."

"I love this book, Ms. Jeffry."

"Thank you. Please call me Jane, if you like."

"Okay, Jane. And you'll call me Annie. I'd like to represent you. But I wanted to tell you how I work before we go any further. I don't expect my authors to sign a contract. I don't work with people I don't think I can trust. I've spoken to Felicity and she says you're honorable."

"That's good of her to say that."

Annie continued. "Most agents used to charge ten percent of what the author earned. In recent years, most have gone to fifteen percent. I stuck with going halfway between — I charge twelve and a half percent. But I also charge for a few other things, like FedExing advance reading copies to reviewers that the publisher doesn't send to. And I write contracts that save the foreign sales for us, when I can. I often send copies of books to overseas publishers as well."

"That sounds fair to me. I'm so new at this that I didn't know what to ask," Jane admitted.

"You'll learn fast. Now — you are writing another historical mystery, aren't you?"

"I am. It's not about Priscilla, though."

"That's good. It's hard with historical mysteries to keep one heroine perpetually involved in murder. When is this one set?"

"Edwardian. I'm still researching. I have a vague outline and the first few chapters — at least I think right now that they're the first chapters."

Jane was surprised at how calm she felt. Annie was leading her through this important discussion with skill and tact.

"I'm sure we're going to work together well. Do you ever visit New York City?"

"I haven't for a long time. But I could."

"I'd like to meet you in person soon. And I'll need a bit about your background, anything you think would interest the marketing people or readers. Could you e-mail me something within the next week? Two hundred words or so."

Jane smiled to herself. This was going to be easy, and it would probably surprise Annie to learn that Jane had grown up all over the world with her diplomat father and her mother and sister. She'd save the story about the French teacher who taught a bunch of twelve-year-olds to pick locks. That would be a good story to tell Annie when they met in person.

"Would the middle of next month be a good time to meet?" Jane asked. "I'll have all my children back in school by then."

"Perfect. We're going to make a great team. I'm so pleased at how professional you already seem to be. I especially liked that you answered the phone saying 'This is she.' Shows that you know your grammar. Let me know so I can schedule a lunch at a very expensive restaurant and a meeting with my staff."

Mel felt obligated to attend Dennis Roth's funeral. Aside from Denny's parents and an elderly aunt and uncle, he was the only other mourner present. It was a short service and a short drive to the old cemetery. Mrs. Roth was stoic throughout both the funeral service and the burial. It fell to Mr. Roth to introduce Mel to the aunt and uncle.

As they all headed toward their cars, Mrs. Roth said, "Detective VanDyne, your people missed something."

"What do you mean?" he asked politely.

She handed him a small blue cardboard envelope with a snap on it. He knew right away what it was. A safety-deposit box key.

"Where was this?" he asked.

"In a pocket you failed to notice in his billfold. We want to know what bank it's in, but you have better resources and staff to find that out. Frankly, we don't want to spend days calling banks."

Mel tried to hide his fury. This was, indeed, a huge mistake. He'd find out who had gone through Denny's belongings and packed them up — and tear a strip off whoever it was. "Let me write down the box number on the key. I'll get back to you as fast as I can. I'm making this my first priority. I'll know what bank it's at and let you know before the day is out."

Back at his office, he assigned four people to divvy up the names of every bank in the city, gave them the safety-deposit box number, and told them to personally call on every bank on their list and report back when they found the right one, which better be today.

Then he went about finding out which

officer had inventoried and boxed up Denny's belongings. He noticed that the billfold was listed. Ten dollars and twenty-seven cents in it. Two credit cards. Two call tags from a tailor, one coupon for a fast-food restaurant and another for fifty cents off on a local dry cleaner. A California driver's license, a picture of his parents with him as a teenager.

A checkbook was also mentioned. Mel went down to where the four officers he'd assigned the chore of finding the bank were convening. He told them to continue but not to start out until he determined where the checkbook was from.

He called the officer who'd boxed Denny's things and told him to come directly to his office immediately.

The officer who'd signed the inventory was there in minutes, looking terrified. "You wanted to see me, sir?"

"Yes, I do. You missed something very important in boxing up Dennis Roth's belongings. Who else was observing you doing this?"

"Another officer, Robert Wilson, who wrote down everything, and the manager of the apartment. Both signed the inventory. What did we miss, if you don't mind telling me, sir?"

"A blue cardboard envelope in a pocket of his billfold. A safety-deposit box key was in it, and there was also a checkbook. You didn't write down what bank the checkbook was from."

"But I remember, sir. I'm sorry I messed up. The bank was the one closest to the college." He gave Mel the name of the bank.

Mel indicated that the officer stay where he was seated, and went down to the workroom where the four officers were still sorting through banks by zip code for efficiency's sake. "One of you start with the bank closest to the college, would you? It might save a lot of hunting."

He went back to his office, where the officer who'd botched the inventory was pacing nervously. "You'll stay here until we know if the safety-deposit box is in the same bank. And you'll do a much better, more thorough job the next time, won't you? You did search all the pockets of his clothing, I see. If it's the wrong bank, you'll join the other four officers still sorting banks by zip code in room 4B."

Chapter Twenty-three

Jane called Mel at his office to tell him about choosing an agent.

He cut her off. "Janey, I'm waiting for an important call on this line. May I get back to you when I'm free?"

"Sure." Jane wasn't offended. She knew when he was this curt, something crucial was happening. Instead she called Shelley to tell her about the conversation with Annie Silverstone.

"You didn't ask what other authors she worked with?" Shelley asked.

"I'll find out eventually. I really liked how she explained her policies. I have Felicity's e-mail address. I'll tell her about this later. Annie wanted two hundred words about my background and interests to send along with the manuscript for Melody to show the marketing people. I need to write it up today."

"Your background is going to surprise them, I'll bet."

"There's another thing I forgot to tell you. Annie wants me to come to New York soon to meet her staff. Want to come with me? We could do some really good shopping and eating."

"That sounds wonderful." Shelley said. "We better set a date and I'll make the plane reservations. Paul has thousands of frequent-flier miles we can use to fly first-class both ways. Have you told Mel about this yet?"

"I tried, but he hung up on me. Something important is going on."

"Did he give you a hint?"

"No. And I didn't dare ask. Are your caterers ready for dealing with a mob? Is it a snack-supper-type thing?" Jane asked.

"No. More like cocktail party snacks. It's later than usual and the students will have time to feed themselves. Not that they aren't welcome to eat. I've ordered extra things that you and I like. Reheatable, so we can bring any extras home."

"Do we need to dress up? I've been wearing jeans or jean skirts so far."

"I intend to be a little more dressy this evening," Shelley replied. "Just because of Evelyn Chance's extra guests who contributed to the college to fund this. Some of them might be businesspeople who know Paul."

Jane interpreted this to mean, at the least, trousers with a good blouse, and a jacket or a light sweater and even a bit of jewelry.

When they finished their talk, Jane went to her front hall closet, the staging area for her most recent dry cleaning. She was appalled at how many things were in there. She broke down and hauled them all upstairs, ripped off the flimsy plastic, and put them in her bedroom closet, pulling out a pair of good black slacks, a matching jacket, and a pink-and-white-striped shirt. Then she went to her jewelry case to rummage. There was a pinkish opal pin surrounded by silver filigree that needed polishing. And a matching ring. These would look good if they were clean, but she didn't want to waste time polishing them up. She'd just wear her best watch.

She went to the computer station she'd set up on a secondhand small desk that she'd actually refinished herself — almost competently. She wrote up her bio and figured out how to do a word count and was shocked to discover that the bio was 427 words long. There wasn't anything she wanted to cut. And it wasn't as witty and charming as she'd expected it to be. She didn't even save the file. She'd have to start over.

As she rose from the desk to pace

around the bedroom while she mentally composed a better bio, she spotted Max, her black, white, and gray cat — the equal-opportunity shedder — washing his paws while reclining on her black trousers. At least he hadn't started to sharpen his claws on the fabric.

Mel called the Roths' hotel number and said, "I have a court order from a judge to open your son's safety-deposit box. I'm sorry it took me a while, but it was the only way to do it. Neither you nor your wife are signers on the box, so I have to use the document and key. Would you like to meet me at the bank around the corner from the college campus?"

This question flummoxed Harry Roth. He had to write the directions down to the last detail. "I suppose we should be there. I can't imagine what was so important to Denny to hide it away like this. But Aggie and I would like to know. And close out the box so we're not billed."

Mel was surprised that the cost of the box was as great a concern as what was in it. For people who could take month-long vacations, the price of a safety-deposit box shouldn't have mattered.

The bank employee put in her key and

turned it. Mel did the same with one that had been found in Denny's billfold. The bank employee left the room.

Mel pulled a bag of latex gloves out of his briefcase and cut it open.

"What are you doing that for?" Mrs. Roth asked.

"Fingerprints. We have no idea what documents are in here. I'll have to look at them first, if that's all right with you." His tone made it clear that this was the way it would be done no matter what their answer was.

Harry said, "It's okay with me."

Mel pulled out the small box, took one of the enclosures, opened it, and pulled out two folded pieces of paper. He opened the smaller one with a pair of tweezers he'd pulled out of his pocket. He turned to the Roths. "It's his original birth certificate with names of his birth parents. Do you want to read it?"

Harry was firm. "No. We didn't want to know that when we adopted him and we still don't want to know."

Mrs. Roth hesitated, looking at her husband for a long moment. Then said, "I agree. But what is the other paper?"

"It's a photocopy of the same thing. Without the seal. I'll need to keep both of these. If you change your minds sometime, I can provide them to you." He put the documents in a large envelope.

There was another packet at the back of the box — a fat unsealed envelope — which Mel gingerly opened with the tweezers. It was full of cash. He also put this in his envelope. "There's quite a bit of cash," Mel told the Roths. "I'll need to have it fingerprinted before turning it over to you."

"How much cash?" Mrs. Roth asked.

"After it's fingerprinted, I'll have it counted in the presence of myself and two other witnesses and let you know how much it is as soon as I can. Would you like it converted into a cashier's check and sent to you via FedEx with copies of the witnesses' signatures?"

"How will we know that some of it hasn't gone missing before being counted?" Mrs. Roth asked.

"You'll know because I'm not going to steal it. I'm an honorable person."

Mel removed his gloves and threw them in a handy wastebasket. He put the box back into the slot and turned the key, handing it to Mr. Roth.

"You can take this back to the woman waiting outside the room and I'll sign off on the box."

As it turned out, Denny had already paid for a six-month rental and had only opened the account a month earlier, so the woman in charge gave him a refund check, which he made a copy of and signed over to the Roths.

"I'll be back in touch with you as soon as these are processed."

"Processed? What do you mean?" Mrs. Roth asked curtly.

"Studied for fingerprints, as I already told you," Mel replied just as sharply.

He walked out of the bank, already on his cell phone, and left them to find their way back to their hotel.

Shelley drove her minivan to the dress rehearsal because she wanted to see that the cocktail snacks were being set up well before anyone else arrived. She was immediately impressed with this caterer. There were half a dozen workers, all in clean pressed white shirts, black trousers, and red bow ties. They all wore clean white gloves. They had set up several steel containers over Sterno candles. The containers were all lidded.

Plates of cold food covered with plastic wrap were also put out on the serving tables they'd set up, which were draped in the same red as their ties. There was no seating for the guests. But small trash cans were set up all around the perimeter of the lobby. The forks and spoons laid out were of sturdy silver-colored plastic. The head chef was wandering around supervising, reminding all his employees to smile.

Shelley greeted him and asked if she could look behind the tables. The owner himself lifted the draping to show her the shelves below holding extra containers of food.

There were small canapés with smoked salmon, tuna salad, or seared vegetables, topped with tiny blobs of caviar, and an equal number without the caviar for those who didn't like it. Attendees weren't allowed to serve themselves the caviar. There were servings of delicious-smelling sausages with parsley, and several sauces for them in small white dishes with little spoons.

Several of the heated dishes were mixed vegetables cut cleverly, and there was one of Jane's favorite dishes — scalloped potatoes, with a dusting of paprika. In addition, there was a vast assortment of rolls. Some with salt, some with caraway seeds, some with celery seed, and many plain. The desserts were still in the trucks, being kept hot or cold as needed, the owner explained.

The napkins were generously sized and looked almost like real cloth. They were stamped with red stars. Shelley was impressed.

Jane had eaten at home before dressing and arrived shortly after Shelley. She was followed by members of the cast and crew and the honored guests Evelyn Chance had invited. The servers greeted them with smiles and started serving.

"This whole room smells heavenly," Jane said to Shelley. "I've already eaten but the aroma is making me hungry again."

Mel soon arrived, and Professor Imry came last. The doors were then locked to prevent casual pedestrians from joining the party.

A separate table was set up for drinks. Everyone had been given a chit for one free drink, and a list of the cost for second rounds was posted behind the table. Jane used her chit for a Coke. Shelley opted for white wine.

Mel, apologizing to Jane for cutting her short on the phone earlier, went through the buffet line with her. He kept his conversation bland and cheerful, and so did Jane.

For about a half hour, people mingled

and ate, chatting excitedly about the play. Then the serving tables started being cleared, full wastebaskets were replaced with fresh ones, the desserts arrived, and one waiter was dispatched to collect dishes, napkins, and glasses from windowsills where they'd been left. Some of the guests passed on desserts and started going into the theater. The cast and crew had already withdrawn to the back of the theater. The only people left were Jane, Shelley, Ms. Chance and her special guests, and the catering staff. Even Mel had disappeared.

Chapter Twenty-four

They all sat through the dress rehearsal, except for Shelley, who stayed behind to see to it that the caterers cleaned up, and made sure the yummiest leftovers were put in her minivan.

The play had been promoted as a "whimsical 1930s-style mystery," but the only thing approaching humor, much less whimsy, were the remarks that the butler made to the audience. Everybody found them funny. Imry was furious, of course. The last thing he'd said to the cast was that Cecil, the butler, wasn't to improvise.

The costumes looked fabulous and even Jane felt compelled to tell Tazz what a great job she'd done. It was hard to find her. Tazz had deliberately stayed as far away from Jane and Shelley as she could. She hadn't even turned up for the party in the lobby.

Ms. Bunting was by far the best thing about the play. She played Edina Weston with wry dignity and energy, and was clearly the star. John Bunting actually seemed almost sober. He said all his lines without slurring a single word. He didn't have to put his hand on the back of the sofa or his elbow on the mantel to keep himself upright.

Jane knew Ms. Bunting had to have been responsible for this unusual behavior, and wondered how she'd kept him from drinking.

When the play ended, the small audience seemed surprised. There was some muttering. Jane overheard one of Ms. Chance's contributors saying, "This must be fixed, Evelyn. There's no resolution to the plot. Why did the butler murder the younger son?"

Ms. Chance said, "You should have read the script I sent you early on. There could have been a better ending if supporters of the theater had spoken up sooner."

"She can't wiggle out that easily," Jane whispered to Shelley. "She'll probably never get more funding for anything from him."

"Serves her right," Shelley whispered back. "She could have influenced Imry to fix it. She was the only person he had reason to be afraid of."

The curtain calls were interesting. When the characters, in reverse order of importance, came on the stage, Bill Denk, the butler, was cheered, and the clapping went on for a long time — especially considering he had so few lines.

But when Ms. Bunting, elegant and smiling, came on stage, there was a standing ovation. Flowers were brought on stage for her. A dozen red roses.

"We should have sent her flowers," Jane said.

"I've already ordered them for the opening night tomorrow. I wonder who these are from?"

"I'd guess they're from her daughter as a special early surprise. At least I hope so," Jane said.

As they followed the limited audience to the lobby, they overheard other complaints about the unsatisfactory ending of the play. The wives of some of the crew had been present. The prop master had brought along his daughter and her small son, who had fallen sound asleep within the first half hour. The scene painters were allowed to be in the audience with their girlfriends.

Before going home, Jane and Shelley went backstage to tell Ms. Bunting how good she'd been.

In the background, they could all hear Ms. Chance berating Professor Imry. "You're going to have a long night, young man. You're going to have to rewrite that ending. The investors who pitched in to help the college fund this are in revolt. Either change the victim and perpetrator, or figure out an explanation for why the butler would kill the younger son. It makes no sense."

Jane, Shelley, and Ms. Bunting were all smiling at this rant.

Jane had to ask, "Who were the roses from?"

"My daughter. She always does this. Giving me something to enjoy before the actual performance, no matter where it is. She's wonderful."

"We have to go home now," Shelley said, still grinning. "My car is full of leftovers from the party, and I need to get them in the fridge soon."

"Will you be back tomorrow?" Ms. Bunting asked.

"Probably just for the last act," Jane said. "To see how it ends the next time."

They all laughed.

Mel hadn't watched the dress rehearsal except for the last scene. He'd been at his office tying up some loose ends on another case that had just cropped up that afternoon. It involved one of those stupid criminals who didn't leave the scene quickly enough.

A skinny, weedy young man had burgled a house and walked out the front door with all the family's silver in a burlap bag. There he was confronted by the burly owner of the house, who had a big loop of rope he was going to use to make a swing in the backyard for his kids. The guy tied the perp up with the rope while his wife called the police to fetch the burglar.

Mel got the call and told one of his assistants to go pick up the bungling burglar. Both of them had a good laugh over this.

He was still chuckling to himself when he arrived backstage after the last scene and heard Ms. Chance threatening Professor Imry. He waited in the hall until she'd gone, then went into Imry's office.

"I have something important to tell you. You better sit back down," Mel said.

"Okay. I guess it's that you're going to arrest me for murdering Denny, which I did *not* do! That's the way my day's gone. Are prisoners allowed to take their laptops into a jail cell?"

Mel had to suppress a smile. Imry had been inadvertently funny, probably for the first time in his life.

"I'm not arresting you," he said. "But I

do have bad news for you."

Imry ran his hands through his hair. "Hit me with it."

"Understand, Imry, this is absolutely confidential. I'm only telling you this because I feel you need to know — but you have to agree not to mention it to anyone, not even obliquely."

"Okay. I'll pretend we never spoke of this."

Mel told him what he'd come to warn Imry about, and Imry turned so white and pasty that Mel feared he was going to faint.

So Mel added, "But I have a suggestion for how to solve the problem you're going to have."

Shelley was desperately anxious to get home before any of the food spoiled. She hauled in all the leftovers and put them on Jane's kitchen counter. "You pick what you and your kids most want, then I choose something, then you take another turn."

"Shelley, that's insane. You paid for all of it. You take everything you want. Just leave us whatever is left. By the way, is tonight's catering service on your list to provide meals for Paul's dinners?"

"Absolutely. They were fabulous. It's sort of discouraging that out of the ten I tried out, only two made the grade. I was hoping that at least three or four would be acceptable."

"Poor Professor Imry," Jane said out of the blue. "Having to rewrite the whole last scene overnight."

"I don't see how you can feel so sorry for him." Shelley was outraged. "He was simply too arrogant about his work to do the ending right. Or maybe too lazy. Or incompetent. I'll bet you good money he's never opened the first page of a good mystery book."

"Shelley, I'm seeing this from a different view. If I'd messed up an ending and had to fix it overnight, I'd probably just go to bed and hope for the best."

"No, you wouldn't," Shelley said. "You'd fix it."

"I guess I would. Now let's sort out this food choice thing. My kids will eat anything. Except that none of us likes caviar. Does that help?"

Steven Imry was still fixing the script as dawn broke on Friday. Now there was no murder, just a threat of one. And the younger brother didn't die. He just ran off with Angeline. After which his older brother Todd, now played by Norman

Engel, admitted he was relieved. Imry knew, deep in heart, that this wasn't the best ending. But hoped it would satisfy the horrible Ms. Chance, her investors, and the audience. It was at least upbeat.

Best of all, only two of the actors had to learn new lines before tonight. Norman and Jake Stanton, both of whom were fast studies.

He printed out several copies of the new ending of the script, and paced around until eight in the morning, when he called both the actors involved in the changed script to tell them to meet him at the theater at nine promptly. Meanwhile, he'd have to contact the rest of the cast to tell them about the changes, so they wouldn't be surprised at the last minute.

At least he hadn't been forced to fix the script in a jail cell.

Chapter Twenty-five

At a quarter after ten Friday morning, Ms. Bunting called Jane and said, "I hope I didn't interrupt your writing. I meant to call Shelley, but I've lost track of her telephone number."

"Here's her phone number," Jane said, rattling it off. "You didn't interrupt anything. I was just catching up on laundry. What's up?"

"I've finished my needlepoint project and called the shop to see if they'd finish it as a pillow."

"I think Shelley has finished hers as well. I'm not quite done with mine, though."

Ms. Bunting said, "When I talked to Martha, I asked her if she could show me this basket-weave stitch so I can start a new project. She said she'd be free at one o'clock to teach all three of us, if we wanted."

"That's wonderful. I want to go along as well. Can we give you a ride?"

"That was what I was about to hint at," Ms. Bunting said with a laugh. "John is still wasting time hunting for his golf club, and I don't want to take a cab. My last ride in one was harrowing, to say the least."

"I'll give Shelley a call and tell her this. We'll pick you up in time to be at the needlepoint shop at one."

Shelley was delighted. "I *have* finished my sampler and want to have it framed and then pick out new thread colors for this basket-weave project."

Jane laughed. "You just want to fill up more of the pockets in your jewelry holder thing. So do I. We still have thirty more pockets to fill with pretty colors."

They picked up Ms. Bunting, who was waiting in front of the hotel. "This is so nice of you girls to haul me around."

"You merely inspired us to go spend money," Jane said.

"It could turn into an expensive hobby, couldn't it? But well worth it," Ms. Bunting said. "I've already completed one in two weeks, and the play runs another three. I'd be bored senseless if I didn't have something do with my hands all day."

When they arrived, all three of them bought new canvases and new threads in gorgeous colors. They also learned how to do basket weave.

Martha gave them each a scrap of leftover canvas and showed them how to do the stitch. "Remember, keep a loose hand. This is the most durable of the patterns, but it will go all diagonal if you do it too tight."

Ms. Bunting said, "You know, I was a little afraid at first that I couldn't do needlepoint this well. I have a touch of arthritis in my right hand. I was surprised to learn that the stitching was good for me. The pain went away after the first few days. It's been good for me in a number of ways."

"I'm so glad to hear that," Martha said. "I've heard the same from other people new to needlepoint. Sometimes it makes that big muscle in your thumb hurt a little for the first few days. But all three of you have mastered the right tension," she added, looking at the projects they'd brought along.

"Will you be able to turn mine into a pillow before the play is done?" Ms. Bunting asked.

Martha said, "I normally send it out to be done. But for you, I'll do it myself. Let's look over fabrics that you'd like for the back and the piping around the edges." She proceeded to rummage in one of her storage bins and spread out a dozen or so swatches.

"I like the Wedgwood blue," Ms. Bunting said. "Is it sturdy enough?"

"It's the perfect weight and heft. I have enough of it, and I can have the pillow ready for you early next week." She paused a moment, then added, "Mrs. Nowack, you're doing that basket weave just a tiny bit tight."

Professor Steven Imry called Evelyn Chance at eleven-thirty Friday morning and told her how he'd changed the script, explaining that only two actors needed to know different lines in the final act and they'd already rehearsed it.

"I want to see it myself," Ms. Chance said.

"Then pick up a copy in my office at the theater. I'm going home to sleep this afternoon." He hung up.

She called back, furious, and there was no answer.

Mel called Jane and asked, "Are you two going to the opening night of the play this evening?"

"Probably not for all of it. We've already seen nearly every scene, except the one Evelyn Chance insisted that Imry change. We might show up at the end, though, just to see if it makes sense."

"I hope you will. And Jane, this is going to be an imposition, but would you and Shelley hang around for a bit after the play?"

"I suppose so. Why?"

"I can't tell you. But I'll need both of you there."

"Okay." Jane was perplexed but knew better than to argue.

She called Shelley and repeated the mysterious message.

"What on earth would he need us for?"

"Maybe to give some sort of information about the murderer?"

Shelley said, "We don't know anything worthwhile. What little we do know is about Ms. Bunting, and she's certainly not a murderer. But if he wants us there for some obscure reason, I guess we should do as he asked. Have you told him about your agent yet?"

"I haven't had the chance. He's been too busy. I don't want to give my good news to a man too preoccupied to fully appreciate it."

"We might as well turn up for the whole play," Shelley said.

"Oh, please no, Shelley. I couldn't bear it."

"Okay, but I'm going to go to see how the college handles the intermission. They might have a caterer that I don't know about."

"I'll join you then as a taster," Jane said, "and sit through the last act to see if Imry's fixed it."

Jane dutifully showed up and was horrified to see how hard it was to park anywhere near the theater. There must have been a good turnout. She supposed that all the drama students were forced to attend, as she had been when she was taking a similar course in college.

The catering at the intermission was, in Shelley's opinion, not good enough to even ask who they were. She told Jane that the wine was cheap, the canapés weren't very good quality, and the paper plates were flimsy. Jane, having accidentally lost her grip on her plate and dumped her too-dry tiny sandwich on the floor, agreed.

They could only find seats on the far side, two-thirds of the way from the stage. The sound wasn't very good where they sat, but they sneaked down and stood in the aisle to hear the resolution in the final fifteen minutes. It was okay. Not really good, but acceptable. When the actors came out for bows, only Ms. Bunting provoked a standing ovation.

Jane and Shelley knew a semi-secret way to get back behind the scenes by now without attracting the attention of anyone in the departing audience, though they discovered that quite a few other people also knew the way. The cast was still on stage. Ms. Chance and some of her benefactors were already backstage. So were some of the students of the drama school. A few of the crew members and their families showed up as well.

"We'll just stand around until the crowd clears," Jane said. "Mel will find us when he needs us."

Eventually the crowd thinned. The actors returned to the dressing rooms to remove their costumes and makeup, some with haste because they had a free weekend to enjoy, since the next performance wasn't until Monday night.

Mel finally showed up. "We're having a meeting shortly in the workroom. Go wait in there, if you would," he told Jane and Shelley.

There were three people already there whom Jane and Shelley had never seen. One woman and two men. None of them showed any interest in Jane and Shelley nor each other.

Jane and Shelley took seats at the foot of the table and didn't speak a word. Nor did the two men and the woman. Professor Imry was the first familiar person to show up. He took his usual seat at the head of the table. Five or six minutes later Ms. Bunting came into the room and sat next to Imry.

She said, "What is this about? I'm tired and want to go back to the hotel."

Imry looked past her as Mel and John Bunting entered the room.

John already had found a drink to bring along. "What's going on here?"

Mel closed the door behind him and said, "I'm here to arrest you for the murder of Dennis Roth."

Bunting spilled his drink. "That's crazy! I did no such thing." He glared at Mel and asked, "Who are these strangers?" indicating the two men and the woman.

"The men are plainclothes police officers who are going to escort you to jail. The woman officer will stay with your wife."

Mel read Mr. Bunting his rights as one of the men handcuffed him.

"Take Mr. Bunting away, please."

Shelley and Jane turned to Ms. Bunting. She was pale, but almost as composed as always. "Did he really do it?" she asked Mel in a voice that barely wavered.

"I'm sorry to say he did," he replied.

The policewoman sat down next to Ms. Bunting and offered a tissue, which Ms. Bunting waved away.

"I asked Professor Imry to sit in to assure you that the play will continue," Mel said. "The young man who plays the old butler will take over your husband's role. Professor, please confirm this before you leave."

Imry did so, then left the room after apologizing profusely to Ms. Bunting.

"What is the evidence for this?" Ms. Bunting asked.

Mel pulled up a chair from the table and turned it around to face her. "There is a lot of evidence. Are you sure you want to know all of it?"

"Yes, I do," Ms. Bunting said.

"The missing golf club was found by a well-known Dumpster diver two blocks from your hotel and pawned. There was blood in the grooves on the flat head matching Dennis Roth's DNA."

Ms. Bunting closed her eyes and took a deep breath. "Go on."

Chapter Twenty-six

"I hardly know how to put this in the right order," Mel admitted. "There are a number of confirmations. The Dumpster diver knew what day he found the club and pawned it the day after the janitor was struck. There was a bellman at your hotel the same day who saw your husband walk out with a golf club in his hand and return shortly later without it. The only reason he remembered this is because it was his last day before a short vacation, from which he returned today."

"Anything more?"

"Yes. Sven Turner, the college janitor who was attacked, has recovered his memory. Due only to his sister's determination," Mel said, looking at Jane for a moment. "He was in the audience tonight in a wheelchair in the aisle closest to the stage and clearly remembered that your husband's distinctive voice is one of the two he overheard just before Denny was murdered."

He went on, glancing at his notes. "In addition, we've seized the recent records of the pharmacy his old friend owns. There's a prescription that was given your husband for the same sleeping pills that were found in Dennis Roth's blood system. The doctor's name was forged by your husband's friend. He's going to be in trouble, too."

Ms. Bunting was quiet for a few minutes, and finally said, "I'm forced to believe you, but I have no idea why John would have done this. He's not a moral man, I've known that for years. But murder? Why would he murder a perfectly innocent stranger?"

As Ms. Bunting spoke, Jane rose and went to sit next to her.

Mel said, "In Denny's wallet, there was a safety-deposit box key, which was unfortunately overlooked by my staff, but found by his adoptive parents. In the box at the bank was Denny's original birth certificate and a copy of it with your husband's fingerprints on it." Mel paused for a long breath before saying, "The birth certificate named his birth parents, Susan Thayer and John Bunting."

Ms. Bunting drew a sharp breath. "Susan Thayer? I know that name. We did a play here in Chicago about twenty years ago. She had a small role in it. She was not a nice young woman. I remember, too, that

John claimed he was spending a lot of time with all his old school friends. I suppose now that was just one of his many lies. He must have been with her."

Gloria Bunting finally broke down. Her voice was clogged with horror and tears poured down her face. "It can't be John. There must be other people with the same name."

"A blood sample will be taken as soon as your husband is booked. Of course, you could be right. However, there was also two thousand dollars in the box. Your husband's fingerprints were on the first and last bill in the stack, and so were the fingerprints of his pharmacist friend. The pharmacist admits to lending the money to him because your husband told him he was being blackmailed by an illegitimate son."

The woman officer offered Ms. Bunting a tissue again. Gloria took it this time and dabbed away the tears and blew her nose. "Thank you, miss. Detective VanDyne, I hope you're wrong. But I know in my heart that you're right."

She turned to Jane and threw herself into Jane's arms.

Jane was sniffling as well. "Ms. Bunting, I wish there were some way to help you."

A long moment went by, and Gloria

Bunting mumbled into the collar of Jane's blouse, "You girls find out who is the best divorce attorney in town and make me an appointment for Monday morning."

She straightened up and the officer handed her another tissue. Ms. Bunting's nose and eyes were red, but she was back in control. "Detective VanDyne, I have our only checkbook in my purse. I'm not making bail. Tell John that. I'm not paying his legal fees either. He's going to have to try to get those from his golfing pals."

Shelley said, "We'll take you back to the hotel, Ms. Bunting, and stay as long as you want us to."

Mel said, "That's a nice thought, Mrs. Nowack, but Officer Tanner here is prepared to take you to the hotel, if you like."

Ms. Bunting said, "I'll accept that offer, thank you, Detective VanDyne. I don't want to impose more than I have to on Jane and Shelley."

"What about the play?" Shelley suddenly said in spite of herself. "Oh, what a trivial thing to ask. I'm sorry," she said.

"It will go on," Mel said. "I warned Professor Imry in advance what was going to happen and swore him to secrecy. The young man who plays the elderly butler will take over Mr. Bunting's role. And someone else will fill in as the butler, which is a minor part of the play without many lines to learn. Of course, you won't be expected to perform on Monday night —" Mel started to say to Ms. Bunting but was cut off.

"An actor never abandons a commitment to a role he or she has agreed to do. Unless, of course, they're in jail. I'll finish my obligation. Officer Tanner, I'll just get my purse and come with you."

When Ms. Bunting and Officer Tanner had gone, Mel said, "I'm sorry to have subjected you two to this. But I knew she would need friends present. More than ever before in her life. And you've been good friends to her."

"We'll continue to be as long as she needs us," Shelley said, and Jane nodded agreement.

Mel got up and said, "It's time for all of us to go home. I have more to tell you, but not tonight. We'll talk again tomorrow — I might have to make a hard decision eventually, and I'd like your advice."

"What decision?"

"That rests on a DNA match with Bunting and Denny. Which I'm quite certain there will be. But I'll tell you more tomorrow."

It wasn't until late afternoon Saturday that Mel had the free time to talk to Jane and Shelley.

"The DNA tests won't be in for a while, but it seems that even Ms. Bunting realizes that the other evidence is enough to get a conviction. She's really a tough old lady, isn't she?" Mel said.

Jane, Shelley, and Mel were sitting outside at Starbucks again. It was overcast and a little windy, and nobody else was nearby.

"She is," Jane agreed. "We've already asked Bitsy Burnside who her divorce attorney was. He took her husband to the cleaners. We've given her two other names as well if she doesn't like him."

"I still have a problem to deal with and need your advice," Mel said. "It's Denny's parents. The ones who raised him."

"What kind of problem?" Shelley asked.

"Both of them have told me they never wanted to know who his biological parents were and still don't want to know. So how do I tell them whom I've arrested? And that their beloved son had his original birth certificate and was blackmailing his biological father without telling them who the father was?"

Jane and Shelley looked at each other,

and Jane said, "You probably wouldn't have to give them the name, but you would have to tell them the motive, wouldn't you?"

Shelley said, "Maybe they wouldn't believe it."

Mel said, "That's a lot of help."

"Mel," Jane said, "you're going to have to wait for the DNA results anyway to be sure. Then contact them and sort of feel your way through the conversation. They deserve to know the truth, but may not want to. Let them ask what they want to know."

On the way home, Shelley said, "I'm wondering about something I think is too bizarre to even mention to anyone but you."

"I love your most bizarre ideas. Shoot."

"Okay. Since John Bunting got the forged prescription from his old druggist friend, what else might he have gotten under the table years ago?"

Jane thought for a moment. "Something to create a miscarriage? Or even three of them? Jeepers, Shelley. My grandmother told me there used to be a woman in town who grew rue plants to give girls who were 'in trouble' to get rid of unwanted pregnancies. She said that some part of the plant, crushed up, could do that."

"Which part?"

"I don't know. She didn't go that far. Maybe the flowers, or the leaves or the roots. Or it could just be an old wives' tale."

Shelley actually slowed down the minivan and pulled into a parking lot and came to a full stop. "Should we tell Ms. Bunting this?"

"No. She's as smart as we are. And if the miscarriages happened when they were in or near Chicago, instead of Europe, when she *did* carry to full term, she's capable of figuring this out herself. Especially since she knows what her husband and his drug-gist friend did recently. She knows how to use the Internet; she could figure this out. In fact, I was looking up herbs once, and think I ran across a warning about rue regarding the various dangers of it. Something about mucous membranes."

"I can't believe we're sitting here in the parking lot of a Wal-Mart talking about mucous membranes," Shelley said with a shudder. "So we won't mention this to her. Unless she wavers about the divorce."

"Shelley, she's never going to waver on that."

They attended the play one last time on

Monday. With the changed ending and with Bill Denk doing a magnificent job of playing the role John Bunting had previously held, it had turned into a better play.

Ms. Bunting was just as good, if not better than she had been in the first performance. They went backstage to visit with her and compliment her performance, which again had been greeted with a standing ovation.

"You did good!" Jane said, giving Ms. Bunting a hug. "Would you like to go out to a late supper with us?"

"I'd love it. I'll even pay for both of you. I'm so pleased with the lawyer you recommended. The papers were delivered to the jail the same day. Give me ten minutes to get out of this dress and makeup. I'll meet you in the lobby."

After they'd ordered their drinks and meal at the restaurant they'd taken her to before, Shelley said, "I hope this isn't tactless, but are you going to the needlepoint class tomorrow morning? We can pick you up if you like."

"Of course I'm going. That's sweet of you to ask." Ms. Bunting was cheerful. "I should have divorced him decades ago. I feel so darned independent knowing my life is now entirely in my own hands. I can take any role I want to. I can needlepoint. I can spend time with my grandchildren whenever I like. And the first thing I'm doing is selling our house in Connecticut and purchasing one here. The second thing is getting a better laptop and a fast line. In fact, I was online and looking up things on the Internet yesterday about miscarriages since I learned about John and that horrible druggist friend of his, and you wouldn't believe what I learned. There's this common herb called rue . . ."

Epilogue

Gloria Bunting sold her house in Connecticut and purchased a three-bedroom condo in Chicago that had views of Lake Michigan from the living room, her bedroom, and the largest guest room.

As soon as the news of John Bunting's incarceration for murder hit the newspapers and magazines, Ms. Bunting's agent was inundated with queries. Within a year, she'd been a guest star in two highly popular television shows and had three scripts she was considering for Broadway productions. She later learned from several good sources that her ex-husband had been telling everyone in the theater or film business that she wouldn't take any role unless there was a good role for him.

John Bunting was found guilty of murder and received a twenty-year sentence. But even though he was no longer allowed to drink alcohol, he died of liver disease six months after he entered prison.

The pharmacist who'd forged the prescription for the drugs John Bunting used to disable Denny before killing him went to jail for a year for forgery and accessory to murder. When he was released, his family put him in a nursing home.

The Roths, without wasting money to hire an attorney, filed several lawsuits against the Chicago Police Department, Detective Mel VanDyne, and the college that sponsored the play. All were thrown out of court.

Professor Imry didn't get funding for his next script, so he went to a small college in New Jersey and spent his free time reading Agatha Christie, Dorothy Sayers, Raymond Chandler, and John Dickson Carr. He produced two plays and then was sued for plagiarism. He gave up teaching and writing and educated himself about gardening. He set up an "exotic and unusual" vegetable stall next to a mall in Kansas City and is happy making a modest living.

Bill Denk, who played the butler in Imry's play, and then John Bunting's role, was seen in the production by an important local agent who provided actors for commercials. Since Bill, who was actually young, could play almost any age, he made a good living plugging denture paste, Viagra, and newly opened condominiums. He's now moved up to national advertising for hardware chains, resort chains, and luxury cruises.

Sven Turner has recovered slowly but completely. He's gone back to working for the college as a janitor and gambling on the weekends. So far, the IRS hasn't taken any notice of him.

Hilda Turner created a trust with her share of their wealth to fund medical research for children with diabetes. She oversees the trust, which has gained plaudits in the medical field.

About the Author

Jill Churchill has won the Agatha and Macavity Mystery Readers Awards and was nominated for an Anthony Award for her bestselling Jane Jeffry series. She is also the author of the highly acclaimed Grace and Favor mysteries and lives in the Midwest.